I've Known
No War

I'VE KNOWN
NO WAR

S.P. MCLELLAN

Library of Congress Control Number: 2015910175
ISBN: Hardcover   978-1-5035-8118-0
               Softcover   978-1-5035-8117-3
               eBook   978-1-5035-8116-6

Rev. date: 06/25/2015

To order additional copies of this book, contact:
Xlibris
1-888-795-4274
www.Xlibris.com
Orders@Xlibris.com
716604

To the world's finest teammates, the men and women of the
United States Armed Forces

CHAPTER 1

Of course Harbor Lake, Texas, was a football town. Aren't all Texas towns first and foremost football towns? Harbor Lake had a nice football stadium and nice uniforms and a head coach who made double the salary of any teacher in the school. The booster club was filled with parents who spent most of their waking hours and all their spare cash in the hopes that their team would make it all the way to Dallas for the state football finals. The dream of most of these parents was that Junior would be the star of the state title game and everyone in town and across the state would pat them on the back and give them credit of their son's gridiron success. This didn't make these folks bad people, as parents all across the USA lived vicariously through their children; it was just that the parents in Texas were often a bit more extreme in that regard, and Harbor Lake certainly was no exception. The thing that set Harbor Lake apart from other Texas towns was that the football booster club was not the biggest booster club financially or member-wise. That distinction belonged to the baseball club, the Harbor Lake Diamond Backers.

You see, the Spartans had sent many players to play Division I college football and even a few to the NFL. Who could forget Billie Joe Krueger, who played quarterback at the University of Texas and even won a few play-off games for the San Diego Chargers? If you asked anyone around town about Billie Joe though, they would tell you about the two no-hitters he threw in 1989 en route to the state baseball title. You can still find Billie Joe most nights down at Molly's Pub along with his catcher from the spring of '89, Mickey Morreale, talking about the glory days. The battery from the school's third state title won't bring up that year unprovoked; however, if you ask them about it, be prepared for a long, detailed description of their senior year. Yes, the Spartan Football Stadium had new bleachers every couple of years and pristine turf and a few sky boxes and new goal posts on a regular basis; however, the teams that played on the gridiron for the Spartans had zero state crowns to their credit, which was four less than the boys who had graced Spartan Field in the springs of the past had acquired.

Therefore, it wasn't that the folks did not love football around here. It was just that they loved to brag, and the boys who took the diamond year after year usually gave them a great deal to brag about. Based on the results from the summer league most of the boys had played in during the summer of 2001, there were high hopes as the spring of 2002 rolled around. There was little doubt that the fifth state title trophy would soon be installed in the covered trophy case outside Spartan Field. Not many in Harbor Lake cared about politics unless you were talking about the politics of college football and whether or not Texas or Texas A&M or maybe even Tech would win the Big 12 South this fall. No one disrespected the Baylor Football Program despite their struggles, as many a Spartan had gone to Waco to play baseball. While the president currently in Washington was from the great state of Texas, a lot more people liked his dad, the former president. You see, the forty-first president of the United States could be seen at almost every Houston Astros game, and he would talk baseball with anyone who could get close enough to him or anyone he felt like approaching. The real politics in this town was about which kids would get to start for the Spartans this spring among the twenty players on the varsity roster. Whatever decision coach Jimmy Ferrell made about the Spartan Nine was sure to fire up some parents; but that came with the territory, and Coach Jimmy did not answer to anyone except the Lord Almighty!

Many thought Coach Ferrell was an angry man; however, Jimmy just could not stand anything less than full effort. He had served as a navy corpsman with the United States Marines after leaving Harbor Lake in 1978. He came home four years later with ribbons and many good sea stories, some of which actually had some truth, most of which were completely false. Jimmy knew that he was not good enough to play major league baseball or even play at most colleges, and he was all right with that. What could be better than playing on Spartan Field with your buddies you had grown up with and being in competition for the state title every year?

He loved the esprit de corps among navy corpsman and the US Marines they served with. Yet as much as he tried, he could not shake the love he held for Spartan Field and the town that held his finest memories. The first person he went to and saw upon his discharge was Dickie Baker, the well-respected longtime coach at Harbor Lake who had molded Jimmy into a scrappy all-district second baseman. Coach Baker told Jimmy to enroll at nearby Alvin Community College and then transfer to the University of

Houston. Dickie promised his old player that when he graduated, he would get him a coaching job in the area.

Jimmy struggled a little bit in college as it just did not interest him; however, six years later, he had earned a history degree, and it just so happened that Harbor Lake had an opening. Assistant coach Lamont Horton had decided to take the vacant coaching job at rival Pearville the same year. Therefore, the state champions of 1989 were led by coach Dickie Baker and the assistant coach the players loved to call Coach Jimmy.

In the fall of 1997, Dickie decided it was finally time to move to his ranch in Bracketville and that the spring of 1998 would be his last season. Fittingly, the 1998 team came together and gave Dickie his fourth state championship on his way out the door. The title was largely won on the arm of lefty Woody Shellfout's arm. Due to the fact Woody was a junior, the expectations would be nothing short of a repeat in '99 for the incoming coach. In reality, though, the '98 team had very little talent other than Woody and was, in fact, a testament to what one motivated coach could accomplish. Jimmy definitely had big shoes to fill.

The anointment of coach Jimmy Ferrell as the successor to Coach Baker came as little surprise to just about anyone, although Jimmy seemed shocked himself. Although he knew he would be the head coach "eventually" of the premiere program that Harbor Lake had become, that day always seemed so far away. Jimmy would never be completely devoid of talent at the school, but he saw something in the freshmen of 1998–99 and, in particular, a smart, fundamentally precise outfielder named McClanahan and a an already bulky, slugging first baseman whose full name was Theodore Smith. The coaches in the area had known about him for a few years by then, and like his teammates, they just called the can't-miss prospect Smitty.

Stevie McClanahan and Teddy Smith, in most ways, were polar opposites. Mac loved school and wanted to continue his education in the Ivy League. Smitty had never met a book he liked and had no interest whatsoever in setting foot in another classroom after high school. The dynamic duo knew they would likely go separate ways after graduation, yet it was something they did not really talk about, instead preferring to focus on having fun in the present. Come next fall, Stevie was headed to Dartmouth or Princeton or Harvard, and Smitty, by all accounts, was headed for the major leagues. For the time being, however, the pair had two major interests in common. Number 1 was pursuing a state championship, and a close second, of course, was enjoying every single postgame party to the maximum extent possible.

As their senior year approached in the summer of 2001, not a day went by without an intense workout and a few beers. Regardless of how many beers were consumed the night before, the morning workout was never skipped. In order to avoid regular hassle from their parents, the boys both held part-time jobs; however, they worked as few hours as possible. Smitty pulled in maybe eighty bucks a week delivering pizza for Pizza Troopers, and Mac netted a whopping one hundred a week as an unmotivated busboy at Webb's Cove Restaurant.

After the July 4 weekend of 2001came and went, something seemed to click in Mac. Stevie knew that this was quite possibly his last year of playing organized baseball. Furthermore, he knew for certain that this was his last chance to play alongside perhaps the best player Harbor Lake would ever see. Within a week after Bucky Tucker's Fourth of July bash, the players were working out twice a day and drinking on a minimal basis. The talk from Stevie of Smitty being a first-round pick did motivate Smitty somewhat; yet deep down, Number 5 knew he had a gift that could only be blown by doing something stupid. No, what was really motivating Smitty was the thought of his seeing his best friend getting a shot to play baseball at the college level. Despite the fact, Mac would never admit it—he did not just want to get into a top school. Deep down, he wanted to prove everyone wrong and not only get into a top school but also make the baseball team at a top school.

The other passion Stevie had always had deep inside him was a love of history and an enormous respect for those who had served. His father, J. P. McClanahan, had enlisted in the Marine Corps in 1964 and certainly had no idea at that time of the quagmire SE Asia was about to become. All JP really wanted was to save some money for college and to become a high school coach. Four years later, when his initial enlistment was up, JP could not take his discharge and walk away as he had planned. Although he had completed two tours of duty already, he knew that there were things he could tell young marines and corpsmen on a daily basis that could save their lives. Therefore, JP went on to install tough love at the School of Infantry at Camp Pendleton, California, and Camp Lejeune, North Carolina, before finishing his career training reservists full time in his beloved Texas. There was only one person JP wrote from Vietnam, and that was Betty Lou Kupro. The two small-town Texans had no intentions more than remaining friends, yet the letters they exchanged while Betty Lou was enrolled at Rice University drew them closer and closer.

In 1969, JP returned home on leave from Camp Pendleton and asked the sweet, intelligent Ms. Kupro to become a military wife. Despite the fact the fact the country was turning against the war, Betty was extremely proud of JP, of who he was, what he stood for, and how the marines and corpsmen he served with looked up to him. Mrs. McClanahan could not bear the thought of not raising a child with JP, and they made an agreement that they would go back to Harbor Lake when he retired from the corps and start a family.

In 1984, a lad was born who had his mother's intelligence and his father's work ethic. Stephen Patrick McClanahan would be his full name; however, the rug rat would not answer to *Stephen* for very long. His proud father began calling him Stevie early on, and eventually his mother gave in as well despite her initial objections. It seemed like a fun name, and all they ever prayed for was that their son would be healthy and have fun in whatever he chose to do. JP could not wait for the boy to get older so that they could watch baseball and college football together. In the back of his mind, JP hoped that Stevie might be an exceptional athlete. The old jarhead knew, however, that regardless of what interests his son undertook, the true heroes in his life and his son's should always be not the professional athletes with God-given skills but rather the men he left behind in the jungles of Vietnam.

CHAPTER 2

Over the past ten years, Number 5 had impressed in the springtime on diamonds all over the area. However, in the fall, for the past several years, Smitty had also been turning heads wearing number 44 as a bruising fullback. Smitty loved to tell the story of a hungover morning with Tom Osborne, the legendary coach of the University of Nebraska, on the other line. To this day, Teddy still feels that must have been one of his buddy's just screwing around with him; this is doubtful, however, unless that same buddy could also do a perfect impression of Bob Stoops, the newly appointed head coach of the University of Oklahoma, who called one week later. The two sports stars would also hear from coaches at the University of Texas, Texas A&M, Texas Tech, and elsewhere. Obviously, this attention had to make any teenage guy feel good, yet Smitty knew that eventually he would have to make the decision to give up football and concentrate on baseball. On August 1, 2001, head Spartan football coach Chuckie Chimenti heard a knock on his door.

Coach Chimenti knew that he should not talk Number 44 out of this decision, yet he gave a halfhearted effort to do so. Chuckie had once been a hot prospect himself in the gridiron but put off college in order to join the army rangers, and his knees were never the same. People in Harbor Lake were normally talking football or Houston Astros baseball during the dog days of summer; however, this summer was different as people of all ages were already talking about high school baseball. Unfortunately, they were all about to be dealt a blow they were not expecting, something they would all take personally!

Tuesdays mornings were usually good days during football season in Harbor Lake. By Tuesday the booster club had put behind them a loss the previous week or was even more pumped up than it was on Monday if the team had won the preceding Friday night. Also Coach Chuckie would usually let the die-hards know about any injuries at the weekly booster club breakfast at the Marina Hotel and Conference Center. Chuckie had just returned from that breakfast and flipped on the little portable TV in the coaches' lounge just outside the locker rooms. The first thing Chuckie heard was Diane Sawyer from *Good Morning America* talking about how a plane had hit one of the towers at the World Trade Center. Chuckie turned at that point to assistant coach Marty Rodgers, the resident genius in the high school athletic department. Coach Rodgers was asked to explain "how in the hell any dumb-ass pilot could be clueless enough to not see that huge skyscraper." Marty cleared his throat and was just about to defend the pilot due to overcrowded air space when he saw the second plane hit. At that point, nothing could really be said, and in fact, nothing had to be. It was like a bad movie except that it was, in fact, actually happening. As coach Jimmy Ferrell walked into the room, he was immediately overcome with two emotions: one feeling was sadness for the troops he knew would soon be deploying; the other feeling was what he was sure many other Americans were feeling: he wanted payback.

The inner burning was not limited to the salty old vets at Harbor Lake High School. An Ivy League–bound senior was consumed in the fall of 2001 with a recurring thought of "Why can't college wait?" Stevie Mac kept wondering to himself if he could accept the thought of so many other guys his age fighting in a foreign land while he strolled daily across a serene college campus.

Stevie knew, at some point, he was going to have to mention the possibility of putting off college to his parents, yet that did not bother him. What really gave Number 8 angst was breaking the news to his "brother from another mother," Teddy Smith. Stevie finally saw fit to break the news to Teddy on a Friday night in October. The football team had just scraped out a win against rival Harbor Falls 10–7 minus their former star runner, Number 44. Much as Stevie expected, Smitty's reaction was quick and to the point when he stated, "Have you lost your mind?"

Teddy's first thoughts were of Stevie's future and the opportunities he might be passing up. Quickly, however, his thoughts turned more morbid. What if Stevie were to get blown up? What fun would life be without his best friend? Every dream Teddy had included Stevie, such as Stevie being there for his first major league home run, Stevie going to the World Series when Teddy's big-league club made it, and of course, Stevie standing up as his best man.

Number 5 knew his buddy Number 8 well enough that there would likely be no talking him out of this decision. Since his early days, Stevie had also thought things out and rationalized every decision he had ever made. Everything came down to a series of pros and cons. What this decision came down to was that he would never forgive himself if he did not answer the call to duty.

The next few days, Teddy went through the motions of trying to talk Stevie out of the life-changing decision he had made. As the days passed, Teddy's thoughts became stranger and stranger. The one thought that amazingly kept popping into his head was, why couldn't he just go with Stevie and serve four quick years and *then* go to the majors? Teddy knew he would take grief from anyone he dared to discuss this idea with; however, there was a person in particular he dreaded even mentioning the idea to. That person was a Vietnam vet named William "Billy" Smith, who also happened to be the young phenom's father. As he drove to his father's plant, where Billy worked as an operator, second thoughts consumed him. He drove without the radio on and extremely slow. Teddy wondered over and over what his father was going to say and if he would be angry or perhaps proud.

Billy Smith loved the Marine Corps family and the camaraderie it brought with membership, yet he was still haunted by some of the things he had endured as a navy corpsman in Vietnam. Many young boys just out of high school had given up their lives so others such as him could come home. In the back of his mind, Billy knew he would be proud if Teddy ever chose to be a marine, but he never wanted to see his son suffer the horrors of combat. It was always made clear to Teddy that his family had already given enough, and the youngest Smith owed no further obligation to Uncle Sam. As Teddy walked through the dusty, pothole-laden parking lot of the plant, he braced himself for a "What the hell are you thinking?" Ass-chewing. Instead, Teddy was to receive a counterproposal from his combat-veteran old man.

After Billy received the news, there was the awkward silence that Teddy had grown accustomed to every time Teddy told his dad something he did not want to hear. Billy was not angry though, and in fact, he was not surprised after previously hearing of his son's best friend's intentions; however, he did have one request for his beloved boy. Billy looked Teddy in the eye and stated clearly, "If you have to go in at this time in the world, please tell me you are not going into the infantry."

Unfortunately for the concerned father, Teddy and Stevie had discussed this very thing. They had both agreed that if they were going to do this, then they were not going to do it half-ass. You see, the boys felt that the modern-day air force had its place as a morale booster for the ground troops. The modern-day navy was the world's finest and could launch some fierce attacks from sea when necessary. The coast guard had kicked some ass on the home front in the days following since 9/11 and most definitely had the nation's respect. The US Army had a very impressive history but was just such a large and confusing organization. The boys just loved the fact that two simple numbers could tell any marine's story. For example 2/2 would tell you the jarhead was an East Coast marine from Second Battalion, Second Marine Regiment, and you immediately knew where he had been. The young, buff bucks knew the tradition of Belleau Wood, Iwo Jima, Hue City, and Kuwait and wanted to be a part of it. Teddy and Stevie did not want to play a supporting role but instead wanted to be boots-on-the-ground, tougher-than-nails infantry grunts. As infantry marines and soldiers love to say, "If you are not infantry, then you are just infantry support." In the meantime, however, there was the issue of a state baseball championship to pursue.

CHAPTER 3

The South Texas baseball talent pool had always been rich, and the 2002 season was certainly no exception. Teams all over the southern part of the state as well as teams to the north and the east and even a few out west all had at least one big prospect, and a good number of teams were strong from top to bottom. No single team, however, had a big bopper like Teddy Smith, and no one in the state had his supporting cast.

Harbor Lake had always been a play-off contender and usually advanced very far into the play-offs pool once they earned admittance. The team had normally done this with motivated coaching and kids that overachieved. This year was different, though, and even Coach Ferrell would be quick to admit that you can't create talent. With the big bopper, Number 5, plus the power-throwing lefty, Brad Landry, and the Maddox-like bulldog, Jess Adams, Coach Jimmy knew that all he really had to do was pray these guys stay healthy and out of trouble and they were state tournament–bound.

One of Teddy's major goals for the year was to teach his longtime friend Stevie Mac how to hit a freaking curveball! Teddy, like most people, was amazed that someone who could score 1400 on the SAT was stumped when a pitch had the slightest rotation. Stevie had become a pretty good fastball hitter, yet any pitcher who had done his homework knew that you could ring him up with the deuce. Yet as the season began, Stevie was still hitting the straight ball very far, but pitching machines just can't simulate an Uncle Charlie. Therefore Stevie was still missing badly the first few scrimmages of 2002, and his timing seemed to be going from bad to worse. The embarrassment was then highlighted when Stevie came to bat in the season opener with the bases juiced. Facing Wood Oaks High, one of the state's perennial powers, Stevie approached the plate with runners on all three bases, two outs, the game tied, Teddy on deck, and what seemed like

---

the whole world watching him. All he had to do was walk, and then they would have to pitch to Teddy, but if he failed to get on, then Teddy would have to start the next inning with no one on and could be intentionally walked. Future major league Koby Drabek was having a rough day for him, but his deuce had been working all day. Three curveballs later, Stevie was left standing with nowhere to hide. Most people would forget about the strikeout after Teddy's extra inning homer three frames later, but Stevie would not sleep for several nights and was more and more anxious to depart for the Marine Corps Recruit Depot. When Stevie stopped showing up at the postgame parties, Teddy knew that he had to find a way to teach Stevie to hit an off-speed pitch somehow, someway. Everyone seemed to know that Stevie had a bright future outside of baseball, yet Stevie was just not ready to face that his playing days were over.

As the season went on, the team won more than they lost, and small miracles began to happen in that Stevie was occasionally connecting with curveballs. It seemed that Teddy's motivating talks over $4.99 Busch twelve-packs were beginning to pay off. Teddy had convinced Stevie that he was not losing friends over his lack of hitting and Dartmouth did not give a damn about his batting average. A calming feeling eventually began to settle in with Stevie as he realized that his future, even without baseball, was still pretty bright.

The Spartans lost a tough, well-played game to end the regular season to archrival Kemah Creek. The loss meant that the Spartans would not win the district; however, they were still headed to the play-offs as district runner-up and had as much of a chance at the state final four in Austin as anyone else.

The first round of the 2002 play-offs would be no easy task for the Spartans as the Denton Park Deer had a tough lefty in Dwayne Sarver. Sarver was headed to Hawaii on a basketball scholarship but was still angry about not winning a state title in hoops and now desperately wanted a championship on the diamond instead. Big Dwayne was on fire the majority of the night and took a 2–0 lead into the sixth inning. At that point, he plunked Gary Looker, the Spartan centerfielder, with a ninety-mile-per-hour fastball—not intentionally but just trying to be a little too cute. The next hitter was the quintessential scrapper, Bobby Fishman. Fishman had only two doubles all year, one triple, and zero home runs. However, Fishman did have a high average as he had mustered a crapload of singles. Fishman always choked up on the bat like he was holding on for dear life and never, ever swung at the first pitch. He was annoyingly consistent, and once again, after working to a 2–2 count, he dribbled one through the middle for a seeing-eye single. This brought on Stevie to the plate with a chance to be part of the winning rally. There was only one out, so all he really had to do was not hit into a double play. Stevie knew that even if he struck out, Teddy would get a plate appearance and likely take care of business.

Yet Stevie desperately wanted to put the ball in play and handle things himself. Sure enough, the first pitch was a curve, and Stevie's knees buckled as he was fooled badly. Pitch number 2 was a heater right at the belt, and Sarver got the high strike call. Stevie stepped out, took a deep breath, and prayed that somehow he could at least connect with the ball. When he returned to the box, he knew a curve was coming, and he had a calming moment. At that point, he just figured he was going down swinging as opposed to just standing there looking. The pitch came, and as expected, it was a deuce. As his nervous father watched, much to father and son's relief, Stevie launched the ball to deep left center, and before Stevie had a chance to exit the batter's box, the ball was landing in the ditch behind the left field fence. To say Stevie was stunned would be a huge understatement. Mac tried to make his legs move; however, his head wanted to enjoy the moment. Stevie had never shown up a pitcher, and he certainly did not want to start now. As he ran the bases, his legs felt like lead. He tried to compare the feeling to his last home run in his mind, but he simply could not remember when his last home run actually came. Was it tenth grade, or did he have one last year? He knew he had laced quite a few doubles down both lines but could not remember actually clearing the fence any time recently. When Mac finally made it back to home plate, he was greeted by his best buddy, Number 5, who had a smile across his face as big as Texas.

Smitty said to his friend, "See, I told you hitting curve wasn't that hard, you dumb son of a bitch!"

The first game of the next round of the play-offs, things returned to more of a sense of normalcy—other players setting the table for Teddy and Teddy coming through. In game 2 of the series against scrappy Sam Houston High, the Apollos elected to walk Smitty twice. Batting behind Smitty, however, was the Division I–bound lefty pitcher Brad Landry. Landry was headed to Texas Tech because of his left arm, but he put the ball in play with his bat more often than not. Both times, the Apollos threw four straight balls to Smitty, Landry found gaps in the outfield, and drove Number 5 in. Next up was Jason Lebeouf, who had just moved in last summer from Houma, Louisiana. Lebeouf had zero power but had an uncanny ability to chip balls over the shortstop's head for singles. Staying true to course, Lebeouf slapped singles in back to back at bats and brought up Landry both times with runners on. Landry brought the boys around with a gapper double and another double perfectly placed down the right field line. A couple of two-run innings was all Jess Adams would need as the Spartans held on 4–2. Landry had taken the mound in the series opener, and the southpaw had baffled Sam Houston High, holding them to three hits and one run. So before they knew it, the boys had advanced with a two-game series sweep and were one step closer to Austin.

Next up for the Spartans was the Stratwood Cardinals in the area round. Stratwood had money and first-class facilities and always had a few prospects. This year they were led by a stocky flamethrower named Kirk Pryor. Kirk was headed to the University of Texas on a full ride and then eventually was likely headed to the majors. Going into a play-off round, both opposing coaches had to agree to a "best of three" format. Otherwise, the teams played a single game. The Stratwood coaches knew that their best shot to eliminate Harbor Lake was a single game, and that's the route they went. Landry was rested for the Spartans; however, he would be facing one of the state's best in Pryor.

One of the most important factors in any team making a play-off run is health. Up until the forthcoming regional semis round, the Spartans had been injury-free from top to bottom. The truth of the matter was that one of their hotter players was sick big time and was not telling anyone. The team's smartest player (Number 8) had an ailment that wasn't too macho. Stevie began noticing blood in his stool as far back as October and thought that he had just ingested too much bargain Busch Light Beer. Yet as week after week went by, Stevie knew that he had some type of intestinal disorder.

Maybe it was nerves, maybe he was lactose intolerant—he would find out eventually, but not now, not in the middle of the play-offs at the culmination of his senior year! It was getting to the point, though, that Number 8 was going so often, he could barely walk. Not many people noticed other than Number 5. Teddy continued to give Stevie evil looks every time he came out of the bathroom. Number 8 was getting worried that not only would he not make it through the play-offs but that his Marine Corps plan could be in jeopardy. What would he do if they rejected him when his heart was 100 percent committed to being a jarhead?

Stevie began fighting his affliction with Pepto-Bismol, and that seemed to help for a while. However, eventually it seemed that almost any type of food would set him off, and he began ingesting Imodium like it was candy. As the game with Stratwood began, the tightness in Stevie's stomach was becoming unbearable. Stevie made it through one at bat in which Pryor made him look foolish, striking him out on four pitches. By the time Stevie's next at bat came around, he knew he was doing the team more harm than good. At this point, Number 8 knew the inevitable had come; he then clutched his stomach, nodded at Coach Ferrell as if to say "This is it," and then walked out of the dugout into the waiting arms of his dad, JP. Not a word was said as JP just put his arm around his beloved son, and they walked together to the parking lot. JP was so disappointed for his boy but could not let that show. The only thing that was said between them on the way to the Saint John's Hospital Emergency Room was "Stevie, there is nothing more important than your health. You did everything you could!"

CHAPTER 4

Stevie awoke the next morning with a large scar on his abdomen after having a large section of his large intestine removed. The doctors went in thinking that the athletic teenager simply had appendicitis. However, as it turned out, he actually had infected intestines. Dr. Davis, who completed the surgery, told Stevie when he awoke that he probably had swallowed too much of the wood from toothpicks in addition to the gum he constantly consumed in the dugout.

The first visitor outside of his family that Stevie received was, strangely, not Teddy but, instead, pitcher Brad Landry. Although Teddy did not want anyone to notice, Brad told Stevie that Number 5 became pretty emotional after Number 8 departed. Teddy had always planned to win a state title *with* Stevie; now he was determine to win a title *for* Stevie. Brad had been in Stevie's room for a good twenty minutes before he finally got around to telling Stevie who won the game. Landry eventually explained that somehow, someway, he had outdueled Pryor to a final score of 2–1. The big blow for the Spartans was a two-run double from Number 5 that sounded like it was shot from a cannon. According to Brad, the ball almost went through the chain-link fence in left center field and bounced back in toward the infield almost all the way to the shortstop.

The Spartans were now off to the regional finals the next weekend; a win in that round put the boys in the state final four in Austin. Stevie had been told he would be in the hospital for five nights and was determined to at least be in the dugout for the next round. The opponent, it had been learned, would be up-and-coming power Dobie High. Dobie had agreed to play a "best two out of three" series, and therefore, all of Jimmy Ferrell's arms would need to be rested, and the Spartans would also need to find a way to replace Stevie's hot bat.

Jimmy now had to play politics again with a pool of sophomores and juniors and their parents as every parent thought their child was the next superstar. Despite numerous calls and e-mails from overambitious parents, Jimmy already had his mind made up to play Pat Gabriel, the quiet, skinny kid who had moved in at Christmas break from Norman, Oklahoma. PG was a laid-back dude who did love baseball but mainly just loved being around the guys. PG was a practical joker and loved to poke fun at his teammates and keep them loose with his dry sense of humor. Of course, it was much easier for him to keep others loose when there was no pressure on him. The Okie had talent; however, he had no expectations to play on a regular basis until next year, or so he thought!

Dobie had two crafty lefties who had put together great years. Chuckie Cox and Bernie Bohanon were both southpaws who had no intention of cracking books at a college as they both saw an immediate future for themselves in pro ball. One advantage that Coach Ferrell felt good about was that virtually all his hitters were right-handed and would get good looks at either lefty's release. On the other hand, Dobie had a lineup full of left-handed hitters to go with their mostly left-handed pitching staff. Because of this, Coach Jimmy decided to give little-used junior lefty Darren Krueger a shot in game 1. Krueger could hit, and he could shoot a basketball; however, he loved pitching and pitching alone. Krueg had made up his mind that if he was going to make it at the next level, he was going to make it as a pitcher or not make it all. Krueg threw hard, but his fastball had little movement, and his downfall was often that he had too much confidence in a very hittable pitch.

When Krueg got the word that he was going to get the ball, sleep was difficult that night. He was excited and confident but also consumed with a fear of not wanting to let his teammates down. When game 1 of the Regional Finals began, Krueg's hands could not stop sweating. He did not want Coach Ferrell to see this, so he stuck a small washcloth from his bat bag into his back pocket. Krueg figured he would sweat off ten pounds during the game; however, he did not care as long as the team got the *W*. The first pitch from Krueg was a cut fastball on the outside corner, and he got the call. He knew if he could get that call all night, things could definitely roll pretty smooth. As the night went on, Krueg developed a rhythm with his curveball and just needed a little bit of run support. As he had so many times before, Teddy provided the needed support in the form of another bases-clearing rocket double to the left field gap. When the game was over, Krueg was more relieved than excited. Walking off the field while exchanging high fives, his knees were still shaking and he was pale. When Krueg slapped hands with Jess Adams, the Spartans' game 2 starter, he could tell Jess was experiencing the same symptom—the overwhelming fear of not wanting to let his teammates down.

Jess Adams was a country boy. He liked to ride bulls, wear overalls and cowboy hats, and hated cars while he loved trucks. Thing is that Harbor Lake was not a rodeo town like his native Midland. Yet a funny thing was happening to Jess as he was "killing time" in high school prior to moving back to Midland; he was becoming a hell of a control pitcher. As H. I. McDonough once said in the movie *Raising Arizona*, "There is comradeship among men in prison that can only be found in combat or among ballplayers in the heat of a pennant race." The Spartans were not playing for the National or American League pennant; however, they were playing for something bigger in their minds, the Texas state championship! As Jess watched the coverage of the budding war in Afghanistan the night before the game, he wondered if he should really be so nervous.

Were the high school baseball play-offs really life-and-death? Jess wondered if the guys over in Afghanistan really gave a rat's ass about high school baseball. Would it really matter to anyone but him if he did not come through on the mound? Jess was not a deep thinker, but he came to one conclusion: wanting to come through for your buddies in any situation, regardless of the stakes, was a good and honorable way to live—in fact, the only way to live!

It was going to be a sleepless night for Jess and the boys, as they knew what going to state meant to the community. They were so close to being a permanent part of the Harbor Lake record books yet they knew the boys over at Dobie were thinking the same thing.

Meanwhile, at the Mainland Medical Center, Stevie Mac was lobbying for a discharge. If his teammates (guys he grew up playing with) were going to punch their ticket to the state tournament, then Stevie was going to be there, hell or high water.

The doctors on duty admired his toughness and understood his situation. However, they really wanted to watch Stevie one more day after his surgery to remove part of his intestines. Perseverance and stubbornness eventually paid off as just a few hours before game time, Stevie convinced the docs to let him go. He looked them all in the eye and promised he would go to an emergency room immediately if he saw any sign of blood from behind or any abdominal pain. On the bus to East Houston, players noticed Jess Adams talking to himself, and it reminded them of Private Pyle in the Vietnam movie *Full Metal Jacket*. He was talking to his glove and looking at no one. If he did look at someone, it was as if he were looking through them, as if he had the one-thousand-yard stare of a combat vet.

The pregame warm-ups seemed to take forever as all parties involved were ready to get the game started and end the suspense. Dobie was a local football powerhouse but was developing a hell of a baseball program. They had some good young arms but were loaded with bats. They had confidence that sophomore Cody Large would keep them in the game, but they were really counting on their 3, 4, and 5 hitters, Ray Flemming, Dakota Brawner, and Ricky Rosas. All three sluggers had plans on playing ball long after high school, Flemming in particular. Flemming had been on fire in the play-offs with four home runs and his confidence appeared to be contagious. Coach Ferrell talked with Jess before the first pitch and told the competitive cowboy that he was OK with intentionally walking one if not all three of the terrific threesome. Jess immediately responded to Coach Ferrell's suggestion in a respectful but stern tone, telling Coach Jimmy that it was just not in his nature. Specifically, he said that he stated that he could not look longtime teammates Stevie and Teddy in the eye if he admitted defeat. This trait could be admirable in many situations; however, it immediately backfired in the first inning when all three hitters ripped doubles in the gap to give the Dobie Longhorns a 2–0 lead. When their turn came around again in the third, Jess threw nothing but junk off the plate to Flemming, forcing him to pop up on at outside pitch. Brawner was more patient and drew a walk, and Jess was forced to swallow his pride momentarily and intentionally walk Rosas before getting the number 6 Dobie hitter to ground out weakly to first. Meanwhile the Spartan hitters were getting on base in succession although they had a zero on the scoreboard.

In the bottom of the fourth, scrappy Bobby Fishman came to the plate and fouled off what seemed to be one hundred pitches before drawing a walk. The pest that Fishman was seemed to irritate the young Cade Large, who laced a fastball—not his best pitch—as hard as he could to the next hitter. The next hitter happened to be one Teddy Smith, who had moved up one spot in the order in Mac's absence. Teddy almost predictably launched the ball 410 feet over the fence in dead center, and the game was quickly even. This chain of events seemed to inspire Jess Adams, who then shot down the Longhorns for the remainder of the game. In the sixth inning, a carefree Bradley Landry stepped to the plate. Landry felt he had nothing to lose by swinging hard as Jess was solid, and Bradley figured that Teddy or one of the other clutch hitters would come through sooner rather than later. In swinging hard as for a gap double or triple, Landry accidentally ripped an opposite field homer to the left field power alley. Number 22 subsequently floated around the bases after his first homer of the entire year. As a lefty pitcher, his arm was his ticket after high school, and he had always been a Punch and Judy hitter. Landry couldn't help but think *If Jess can hold on, then I will be the* man *on campus and in town for a few days. I will be the guy that sent us to state!*

As Jess took the mound for the bottom of the seventh, he saw a familiar face walk into the bleachers, his longtime teammate and friend Number 8 had managed to be released from the hospital, after annoying persistence with the medical staff, just in time to catch the end of the game. As Jess caught Stevie's eye, he just nodded and then turned toward Number 5 standing at first base. With a tip of his head, he motioned to Smitty to look in the stands. As Smitty looked that way, Stevie was just taking a seat in the top row. The two "brothers from other mothers" exchanged glances, and the smiles broke across both of their faces.

Most people in the bleachers were so locked in on the game and the nervous anticipation of a third trip to Austin that they did not notice Steve and his dad, JP, sneaking to the top row on the first base line. All eyes were immediately on the cowboy hurler Jess Adams, who was feeling an adrenaline rush that he had not felt since the last time he went eight seconds on a bull in front of thousands of people. Much to his surprise this opportunity was giving him an even *bigger* rush than bull riding. Jess reared back and made maximum use of the adrenaline and threw nothing but fastballs. His arm could rest tomorrow, but tonight, he was going to hurl with everything he had. With every strike Jess threw, more and more folks noticed Stevie and JP's presence. All of the Harbor Lake faithful could not help but grin as they saw the Macs, and they all could not help but think it was their night. After eight pitches in the seventh, Jess had roped six fastballs that could not be caught up with, and the Spartans stood one out away.

The last hope for the Dobie Longhorns was Mikey Wingo, a bruising linebacker who was moonlighting as a slugging first baseman. Wingo was headed to Texas Tech in the fall on a football scholarship; however, he wanted one last taste of high school glory. Wingo was an all-or-nothing slugger who either crushed the ball or swung and missed badly. The future Big 12 linebacker came up hacking and was late on Jess's first heater by a mile. The next pitch, Wingo figured would be more of the same, and as a result, he dug in and was ready. Sure enough Jess tried to blow another one by, and Wingo's connection sounded like a cannon going off as he launched the ball four-hundred-plus feet down the left field line. The Harbor Lake faithful held their collective breaths as the ball sailed well over the fence but hooked just enough to go west of the foul pole. Jess was bent over at the waist, thinking he had just let the whole town down!

In the bleachers, Stevie felt sick, not due to his recent illness, but instead out of fear for Jess. Stevie and Jess were never tight, as Jess was a bit of a loner, yet Stevie could not help but feel for Jess as a competitor and teammate. Stevie and Teddy both knew that if Jess did not come through in this situation, he would never forgive himself. Coach Jimmy was not big on mound visits, as he normally let his pitchers take care of their own business. Jimmy had not taken a mound visit once in the entire play-off tournament, yet he knew this situation was unique. The team was one pitch away from the state tourney—his first and possibly last chance as a coach and definitely the last chance for all his seniors, including a future rodeo cowboy who happened to have a mean curveball. As Jimmy walked out to the mound, he knew that Jess hated to throw the deuce, as Jess always thought it was unmanly in a two-strike situation. Jess considered a hook to be a junk pitch that you throw for strike 1. Jimmy looked Jess in the eye and said, "This guy benches four hundred pounds and can hit a ball damn near five hundred feet. You can throw your heater to anyone else, but I need you to throw a hook to this guy so we can go to Austin!"

Jess did not say anything but turned to look at Smitty as if to say, "Should I listen to this guy?"

Smitty just nodded at him, and then Jess subsequently nodded at Jimmy as if to say, "OK, Coach, I trust you and will do what you want me to do."

Jimmy then sprinted back to the dugout before Jess had time to change his mind. It seemed as if all the Spartan players and fans were thinking the same thing. All of the faithful were anxious to get the pitch on the way to the plate before Jess's pride got the better of him. Finally, Jess let the Uncle Charlie go with perfect spin. Wingo swung with a hard undercut, but his fastball swing was way over the sinking curve, and with that strike 3, the 2002 Harbor Lake Spartans were on their way to the state final four.

CHAPTER 5

The local pubs in Harbor Lake were happening all night long on this May Friday night as past alumni celebrated their alma mater's now finalized trip to state the following weekend. Meanwhile, the players celebrated at Jess Adams's family property outside of town. One little negative trait that came out of the Spartans play-off run was that none of the boys could attend the senior prom, yet none of them seemed to really care. In addition, what many seemed to even notice (especially the seniors) was the scheduled high school graduation pending scheduled for 24 May 2002, only one week away.

Stevie and Teddy had sworn off dating their senior year, as they both felt that girls were an unnecessary distraction. Stevie had spent a considerable amount of time with the young Ms. Renee Porter his junior year and the summer leading up to his senior year and even in to the fall of the senior campaign, much to Teddy's dismay. Stevie had asked Renee if they could cool things in the spring so he could concentrate on the baseball diamond. Stevie had thought that Renee was OK with this plan of action and that they would pick things up again in the summer after graduation. A major sign that this was not likely to be the case was when Renee attended the prom with someone else instead of attending the Spartans play-off game that very same night. Renee had gone to the prom with Robbie Berry, a popular former member of the swim team, now swimming in college at Texas A&M. Renee had sworn to Stevie that it was no big deal and that he had nothing to worry about. At Jess's celebratory bash after the regional final, Renee spoke the words that he did not want to hear but could sense were coming.

Renee stated bluntly, "You're an idiot for going in the marines when you have a shot at an Ivy League education." For emphasis, she added, "I just can't put up with being with someone with such screwed-up priorities."

As much as Stevie hated to hear these words from Renee, it almost came as a relief. He was not sure how she really felt about him, and this answered a lot of questions. He now knew for sure that he must forge his own path and make his own decisions. And if she did not want to be a part of his future, then it was not meant to be. Shortly after his conversation with Renee, Stevie sought out his compadre Teddy, who was out behind the barn doing shots. Stevie just looked Teddy squarely in the eye and told him, "My second thoughts are over. After we win state, I am going through with it. I am enlisting in the corps."

Teddy quickly fired back, "Well then, you son of a bitch, I am still going with you."

For over forty years, the Texas State Baseball Final Four had been held at Disch Falk Field on the campus of the University of Texas. In the past couple of years, however, the tourney had moved just north to Round Rock, Texas, in the Austin suburbs. The new locale was Dell Diamond, so named for the computer mogul, Michael Dell, who built the stadium to serve as a home to the Round Rock Express, the Triple-A affiliate of the Houston Astros. For the high school players around the state, the field seemed pristine as it was considered the finest minor league facility in the country. For minor league players on their way up in the Astros organization, Round Rock could often be the last stop on the way to the big leagues. Conversely, the Triple-A level could also serve as a final chance for over-the-hill minor leaguers or journeymen trying to hold on and avoid the real world.

None of the four teams from their various regions was thinking about the big leagues on this early June weekend in 2002. Instead, their focus was on trying to win a state title for their towns, coaches, and one another and, specifically, having a memory to cherish for the rest of their lives. The 2002 final four consisted of a longtime West Texas football power, Midland Lee; the Hurst Bell Blue Raiders from the Dallas–Fort Worth Metroplex; Corpus Christi Moody High from South Texas; and the Spartans of Harbor Lake from the Houston area.

The Falcons figured they would draw their rivals from the big D, as in years past, the West Texas Region had played South Texas and Houston had played Dallas. Someone decided at the University Scholastic League to mix things up this year. The UIL was convoluted when it came to football and seemed to change the districts and play-off rules every year but largely left baseball alone. It seemed that year after year, the baseball final four was truly the best four teams in the state, and rarely were mismatches seen on this early June weekend. The boys from Harbor Lake did not know much about the other three teams, as they had been focused on surviving in their own brutal region. As it worked out, the Falcons drew the first-time state attendees Corpus Christi Moody, a school that had produced many Division I athletes in numerous sports but never a team state champion.

Coach Jimmy thought about watching tapes and calling other coaches and taking the cerebral approach to the upcoming matchup with a mysterious opponent but that just wasn't him. Jimmy was a blue-collar guy who let players play and did not overanalyze anything. If a player was screwing up, he would tell them straight up in front of everyone regardless of who their parents were, and if a kid did something well, he would complement them with a nod and a pat on the butt. He knew that this was going to be a wonderful time for these kids, and he did not want to ruin it with grandstanding speeches or BS rules. Jimmy knew that for many of them, this would be a memory they would turn to in hard times, especially the two senior leaders who faced a very uncertain future likely thousands of miles from home.

The team arrived to North Austin on Thursday night in preparation for the semifinals on Friday. Normally, if the boys were in Austin, they would want to go out and enjoy looking at hill country women or just soak in fresh air and be carefree. There would be no breaking curfew tonight as every player knew a good night's sleep was vital and most would try futilely to get at least eight hours of sack time. All of the players were nervous about letting their teammates down the next day, but Stevie was worried about how his next group of teammates would feel about him. Would he ever be as tight with a group of guys as he was with his fellow Spartans? He had heard about the comradeship of the USMC, yet he had heard about people who had gone in and hated it. He had to wonder, was it a personal choice of attitude, or was it luck of the draw with regard to what kind of people you ended up with in your platoon? Oh well, he thought, he had to try. He thought out loud, looking to his passed-out hotel roommate Teddy, who had stopped listening to Stevie's serious thoughts some time ago. Once Stevie had come to peace with his decision, at least for this night, he took a couple of Benadryl and turned his thoughts to the Trojans of Corpus Christi Moody High.

The boys awoke at seven and walked out of their rooms down the outdoor sidewalks toward the hotel restaurant. The sun was bright, and the Texas humidity was already kicking in. The boys were glad that they played the first semifinal slated for 3:00 p.m.: they sure did not want to wait until 6:00 p.m. to take the field. The Falcons were told that they could report to the field at 1:00 p.m. for warm-ups. Coach Jimmy secured a late checkout and also secured all soft drinks. The boys could be in one of three rooms drinking Gatorade or water. They had come too far to cramp up in the state semis. None of the boys argued with this or tried to sneak in a soda, as they did not want to be the one guy who missed the biggest game of their lives to date. The hardest thing Jimmy had to fight pregame was keeping the parents away from the hotel, which got ugly at times. He finally convinced them to stay away from the rooms at least, and so most of the parents loitered in the parking lot waiting to follow the team bus. When the bus rolled out, just about every owned vehicle registered in Harbor Lake, Texas, was following it. There was one exception from the caravan, who preferred to stroll the four hilly miles from the Round Rock Holiday Inn Express to the Dell Diamond. That nervous pacer was J. P. McClanahan, who desperately wanted the Spartans to win but more desperately wanted his son to have a final good game or, preferably, two.

Ever since Stevie was born, JP quit worrying so much about a career or his lot in life but focused solely on making his beloved son happy. Stevie had picked up on this over the years and tried to tell his dad that he should do what made him happy. JP would quickly retort that if Stevie was happy, then his dad was happy. Obviously, his father (like any good father) was worried about his son going in the military and perhaps being sent into harm's way, but that was a worry for another day. Today JP was just thinking about his own high school days, how great the memories had been, and he hoped that Stevie could have the same wonderful moments the next couple days. The time seemed to move backward for the players, parents, and coaches alike until 3:00 p.m. finally came and the first pitch was around the corner.

Home field advantage had been previously decided, with the Houston Region, by virtue of several coin flips, drawing the visitors' dugout in the semis as well as the second game if they could squeeze into the finals. The governor of Texas threw out the first ball as was tradition, and the national anthem was sung by rising Texas musician Pat Green, and with that, the 2002 Harbor Lake Spartans finally took the field.

First out to the field was Stevie, who just could not take the waiting anymore. He was followed closely by the starting lefty Bradley Landry. Coach Jimmy was not thrilled about his starting pitcher wasting energy sprinting out to the mound; however, it was too early to get upset. Plus if they were to relax and play good Spartan ball, then it would be largely based on adrenaline. Landry immediately slowed down and began taking long, slow deliveries and making the most of his ten warm-up pitches. Finally, about the third pitch, Smitty lumbered out of the dugout and began tossing grounders to the infielders. He was rarely, if ever, late out of the dugout; however, he wanted to soak it all in this time in case it was his last high school game ever. For a minute, he thought about the military and the danger he might see and wondered, albeit for a moment, if this could be his last game at any level. *Nah,* he thought, *I have never been that unlucky. I was born to play baseball.*

Landry did not look nervous as he began his windup for the first pitch. Instead, he looked kind of star-struck with a mischievous smile. A lot of guys from the area wanted a chance to start in a state tournament game, and he was getting it and was not going to hold anything back. Landry's first pitch was a rocket, a screaming heater down the middle that the scouts in the stands clocked at ninety-two.

Jimmy did not know the speed of the pitch as he did not have a gun himself; however, he knew immediately that Landry was going to throw his arm out if he tried to throw that hard for very long. Landry was a finesse lefty with a good heater but not a power pitcher by any means. Jimmy did not want to rattle him and visit him after one pitch but instead hoped to catch the pitcher's eye and tell him to hold that pitch back for when he really needed it. Coach Jimmy could not immediately catch the southpaw's eye; however, he then caught his first break when the leadoff hitter for the Trojans, Bobbie Brown, stepped out to adjust his batting gloves. At that point, Landry glanced toward the dugout, and Jimmy gave him the peace sign and bobbed him up and down, indicating that he needed to throw more curves and he needed to hold back a little bit.

From that point on, Landry went back to his bread and butter, the big curve, plus worked in sliders and an occasional moving fastball to mow hitters down. Meanwhile, Moody High's skipper, Mike Florez, elected to pitch around Smitty in his first at bat with no one on. The next time Smitty came up, Hickman stood on first after one of his seeing-eye singles. Florez decided to throw some junk to Smitty and see if he would chase; well, chase he did as he roped a line drive inside the right field foul pole, and just like that, the Falcons led 2–0 in the third. Stevie's first at bat was not terrible; he fought off a few pitches and then hit a hard grounder to short. His next time up, he found himself pressing, wondering how many at bats he might have left in competitive baseball. As a result, he struck out on four pitches in his second at bat and came to the plate in the sixth, 0 for 2. By now the Trojans had brought in big lefty Brendan Winans. They had hoped to save Winans for the state title game Saturday; however, obviously, if they did not win tonight, they would not be playing Saturday, and Coach Florez knew he had to keep it close.

Stevie dug in with two outs and a runner on. He tried to make himself understand that he just had to go play defense the next two innings and that his at bat was not going to make or break the Falcons tonight. Pride is stubborn though, and Stevie came out hacking with his "big boy" swing. His first swing was ugly, and he was nowhere close to the ball. He then stepped out, collected himself, and came back with a more level swing following the heater from Winans straight back. He knew he had just missed it and figured Winans would not try that again. Stevie felt that a hook may be coming, and Winans's curve was definitely a beauty. As soon as the ball came out of the lefty's hand, Stevie could tell it was a curve. With his knees bent and his eyes wide, he stayed back and lifted the pitch beautifully as he connected right on the fat part of the bat. The ball rose quickly and headed for the left field power alley. As he sprinted toward first, he thought it may have a chance, but he did not want to be caught jogging if it did not make it, as he would never live that down. So he sprinted around the bases, just repeating in his head, *Don't miss base, don't miss a base.* He knew that Moody High would be watching intently to appeal if he missed base and therefore nullify the biggest home run of his life. Stevie made it around the bases in seconds, flat out of breath, and received a bear hug from none other than Number 5. They had shared a lot of good memories to this point; however, this one was the best.

With the important insurance runs, Coach Jimmy decided to go with Landry a little bit longer but was on alert to take him out at the first sign of trouble. But Landry was floating on air. There was no way he was coming out of this game. To the nervous Spartan fans in the stands, the game seemed to be crawling by. However, to those on the field, the game seemed to be flying by as they loved every second of the tension. Before the players knew it, the bottom of the seventh was on hand and the Spartans were three outs from making the state final game on Saturday. At this point, Jimmy was faced with a decision. Did he keep Landry in, or did he bring his game 2 pitcher, Jess Adams, in to replace his tiring lefty who had done a fantastic job? The other option he had was to bring in Krueger, the wildcard, who had pitched very little but had done a bang-up job when called upon. Jimmy decided he wanted to save Jess for the final game as he wanted it all, and so did the players. Nevertheless, Landry was all over the map with his pitches now and was clearly not the pitcher he was even an hour before. Landry walked the first batter and then managed to get the next hitter on a laser line drive caught by Smitty. Halfway through the walk, Jimmy had Krueger throwing balls behind the dugout. Landry sensed that he was going to be replaced, and as much as he did not want to be, he knew he had to stall to give Krueger time to warm up. The third batter Landry faced almost took his head off with a liner right up the middle. Just like that, the tying run was on deck, and Coach Jimmy knew it was time to make a change.

Krueg was given ten warm-up pitches, and he made the most of them. He slowly and methodically threw all his pitches and stretched very muscle he could in every direction. He was not really nervous until he looked around at his fielders and saw the intense stares in the seniors' eyes. As Krueger looked around, he could tell what this meant to the guys, especially those who were likely playing their last game of organized ball. With that, he took a deep breath and let loose his first pitch, a perfect curve over the outside corner, and much to his relief, he received the strike call. To the guys behind him, the game seemed to now be in slow motion. They were all so ready for the game to be done and celebrate. Krueger sensed this but did not want to rush his pitches. His curve was feeling good, so he went with it two more times, and the batter never even ventured a swing. It felt like destiny to the Harbor Lake faithful as they were one out away.

The next batter was Victor Sandoval, a long, lanky third baseman who was a wide receiver with offers from a number of schools. Sandoval looked extremely relaxed given the possibility of being the last out in the state semifinals. He calmly took the first curve, which was perfect for the fourth pitch in a row. Sandoval had been watching from the on-deck circle while his teammate took three curves and thought, *surely he is not cocky enough to throw the same pitch five straight times?* Coach Jimmy was thinking the same thing but decided to let Krueg go with his own gut and throw what he was comfortable with. The young hurler thought it over long and hard and then went into his windup, and sure enough, he let the deuce fly. Sandoval was expecting it and smacked it in to left center. Fortunately, it was cut off quickly, and the trailing runner was held to third, but the tying run was only ninety feet away. As much as Jimmy did not want to use him, he knew it was time to bring in his planned final game starter, Jess Adams.

Jess felt badly for Krueg and had not wanted to show any lack of confidence in him by throwing any warm-up tosses while his teammate was trying to close out the game. Jess therefore came in as cold as he could be despite the muggy Texas night. Jess was not mentally prepared to throw tonight as he saving everything he had for Saturday night, but he understood that the team needed him and figured after Saturday, he would have plenty of time to rest. His teammates behind him were more than ready to resume the action and get one more out.

After Jess finished his last warm-up pitch, he took a look around and thought on one hand, he was very lucky to be in this position, but on the other hand, he sure did not want to let an entire town down. Jess just shrugged at that point and knew it was not worth overthinking; he was just going to attack the hitter like he attacked a bull—with no fear. With that, the first pitched was whipped, and it was a hard slider that caught the outside corner. The hitter was Johnny Ramos, a Punch and Judy hitter who reminded Coach Jimmy of his own slap hitter, Hickman. Ramos could connect with almost anything.

Ramos had just graduated second in his class at Moody High and was headed to the Naval Academy, choosing an academy over several Ivy

League schools. The son of a retired first sergeant hoped to serve a few years in the military and then head back to South Texas and coach baseball for all his remaining days. He too, however, knew that a combat tour or two awaited him before he came back home. The good news for him was that he had four years at the academy for the world to hopefully become a calmer place. In the meantime, much like Smitty and Mac, he was just trying to enjoy his last days of true youth and true competition not yet destroyed by corporate dollars. Jess did not know Ramos from Adam and therefore came at him with heater right over the middle. Ramos did not even venture a swing, but he hardly ever did; taking a first pitch was second nature to him. Well, Jess figured at this point, Ramos was going to try to take a walk and laced another fastball right down the middle, and much to his surprise, Ramos took healthy cut and laced a hard liner just to the left of the third base line and, therefore, in foul territory. This turn of events sent Jess's head spinning, and he could not make up his mind what pitch to throw. Finally he convinced himself that Ramos was going to get his best heater, and if Ramos hit it, then hats off to him, but he was not letting this game be decided on a curve. Jess had been in the stretch to hold the runners on, but Jimmy had whistled to him to go into a standard windup now that he had two strikes. Jess proceeded to take the biggest windup he had ever taken and the highest Nolan Ryan–like leg kick he had ever had and whip a laser low and outside.

Ordinarily, Ramos may have taken this pitch but not with two outs and a ticket to the state final game on the line, and therefore, he lunged the head of the bat out toward the where he thought the screaming fastball was headed. The seven young men behind Jess figured there was no way the scrapper at the plate could connect with a ball thrown that fast and on the opposite site of the plate from the diminutive batter, but connect he did, and the ball screamed toward right. But as Jess began to hang his head, he saw the power-hitting first baseman, Number 5, leap as high as anyone had ever seen him go vertically (Smitty was a good athlete but ordinarily had no vertical leap), and everyone in the stadium heard the rocketed ball hit the leather of Smitty's big first baseman's mitt. There was silence as everyone waited for him to come back down on his cleats, but come down he did. The big bat had just sent the Spartans to the final game, not solely with the lumber as everyone expected, but instead with catlike instincts in the field he did not even know he had.

Most of the players were stunned and relieved at the same time and just stood in place. Coach Jimmy finally reached the mound first and hugged Jess and asked him, "Do you have one more game in you?"

Jess quickly nodded and said, "I am ready, Coach. I am ready!"

CHAPTER 6

The final game was scheduled for 6:00 p.m., Saturday, and the Falcons had to make the decision as to whether or not to watch the second semifinal Friday night or go back to the room and get some rest. Jimmy gave the players the option as he was not going to order them to go back to the hotel, but as it turned out, he did not need to. Every player as well as his parents was exhausted from the past day and excited about the day coming at the same time. No one had much of an urge to hit the town or head out and watch another game in the Texas humidity.

The boys went back to their hotel and watched ESPN and movies and kept wondering, was this real? Were they really playing for the state title tomorrow? Some of the gents went out to the pool and talked about the game and their potential opponent tomorrow, but none of them stayed long and to their credit, no one snuck in a single beer. Not this time; Saturday was too important. Speaking of tomorrow's opponent, a battle royal was brewing back in the second semifinal between the Midland Lee Rebels and the Hurst Bell Blue Raiders.

The Blue Raiders were a hitting machine with little to no pitching who tended to beat teams 9–7 or 10–8. This game was going true to course, as every inning, runs were crossing the plate. Going into the fifth, the Rebels led 7–6, and both squads had used nearly every available pitcher. While the Rebels' assault had been a group effort, Jamie Gill had been a one-man wrecking crew with two doubles, a dinger, and five runs batted in for the Blue Raiders. As a result, the Rebels' head coach, Spike Dickey, decided he had to walk Gill for the remainder of the game. Dickey's hope was that he could save his star pitcher, Taylor McWilliams, for the final game on Saturday. Dickey's strategy seemed to work as the remaining Blue Raiders appeared to be flustered and popped up or hit weak grounders in the fifth and sixth. Nevertheless, clinging to a one-run lead, Dickey was forced to warm McWilliams up twice in case he needed to come in, and this boded well for the Spartans who wanted to face a unrested ace.

When the top of the seventh rolled around, the Rebels had one man left in the bullpen, a lanky six-feet-five wide receiver prospect in the fall named Davey Stanton. Stanton had the height to play Division I football and had pretty good speed but just could not seem to put on weight. When it came to baseball, Coach Dickey did not care about Stanton's height, only that he was left-handed and could throw strikes. Stanton mainly thought he was just along for the ride for the state final four and never expected to be used. But he had been solid all year, and the Rebels needed McWilliams for their pending showdown with the Spartans on Saturday night. Stanton took the mound with three outs needed and threw his cut fastball and nothing but his cut fastball. Eventually three straight hitters hacked and made solid contact, but all three liners found gloves, and just like that, the Spartans had a finals opponent. The 2002 Texas 5A High School Baseball Finals would feature the Spartans of Harbor Lake and the Rebels of Midland Lee.

The weather for Saturday was turning cooler, and as Saturday evening approached, it was looking like perfect weather for baseball. With the game scheduled for six, the teams were told they could be at the field by three. The Spartans tried to sleep in, but few were able to. In the late morning hours a group of players congregated at the pool for an hour or so, but eventually, the entire team crammed into Jess Adams's room to watch the movie *Gladiator*. What better movie to watch to get in the right frame of mind for the conquest of state baseball championship? Being a long movie, the boys lost track of time, and the coaches had to round them up to load the bus at two thirty. As the bus rolled toward Dell Diamond, the Spartans could hardly believe they were going to play in the state final as opposed to watching someone else play for the state title. Coach Jimmy was wondering on the trip over if he could do anything cute with the team's warm-up routine, especially that of his starting pitcher, Jess, the hurling cowboy?

As it turned out, the players were not able to do much but light-toss and run wind sprints on the side as pregame activities on the main portion of the field were aplenty. The Texas State cheerleading champions were recognized, as well as significant alumni of the Round Rock Express who had gone on to play for the parent club, the Houston Astros. In addition, a charity softball game took place for approximately an hour, featuring local radio and TV personalities. Fortunately, the weather was cooperating and there was no precipitation, meaning all the traffic on the field was not tearing it up. Finally about one hour before game time, the field was free and clear. Both teams were given thirty minutes each for last minute fielding and batting practice. Jess, at Jimmy's suggestion, went down the bullpen to begin light tossing and getting his arm fired up. The rest of the players tried to keep moving as no one wanted to get tight and pull a hamstring—not now!

The Spartans would be the visitor once again in this game, which was good for the Spartan hitters who were tired of waiting but not great for Jess, who was fired up and ready to go. The Spartans felt relaxed and were feeling good about their chances against McWilliams, the ace of the Rebels staff. McWilliams's warm-up pitches prior to the first already seemed fast, as all in attendance could hear the whizzing of his smooth fastball and the smack of the ball hitting the mitt. He mixed in several curves in his ten warm-up pitches just to show the guys what they had coming. Finally at six-oh-one, the first batter walked from the on-deck circle, and it was time to play ball. The scrappy Fishman dug in and prepared for what he considered the most important at bat of his life.

In textbook Fishman fashion, he quickly worked a 3–2 count and began fouling off pitches; before he knew it, he was up to pitch number 8 and finally found one he could handle and hit a seeing-eye single right up the middle. Coach Jimmy was excited to have his leading runner on but was even more excited to have forced the opposing ace to have thrown eight pitches to a single batter and still have three outs to go in the first.

Next up was Gary Looker, the smooth-swinging center fielder who often had led off for the Spartans in the past. Looker went up hacking and stroked one to deep right center. The ball was caught, but it was deep enough to allow Fishman to move up ninety feet. With one out and a man in scoring position, the Spartans had Stevie Mac coming to the plate and Smitty on deck and were feeling pretty good about themselves. Stevie approached the dish once again with nothing to lose, knowing that if he didn't bring Fishman around, then surely Smitty would. With that frame of mind, Mac went up hacking and missed the first pitch badly; however, with the second pitch, he felt the wonderful sensation of the ball connecting with the sweet part of the bat and the ball jumping into the outfield. Before Stevie even made it to first, the ball had bounced over the fence in left center for a ground rule double, and Fishman was automatically waved home to give the Spartans a 1–0 lead.

Number 5 then walked up to the plate, feeling like the king of the world. An RBI, probably two, seemed like a foregone conclusion. Yet baseball is a very humbling game, even for its best players. As Jeff Bagwell of the Houston Astros always liked to say, "If you fail seven out of ten times, you are still an all-star." So it was the humility that came to Smitty in big way as he missed badly on a slider from McWilliams and hit a dribbler right back to the mound and was thrown out by eighty feet. The next batter was Bradley Landry, who had a sweet stroke when facing pitchers throwing under eighty or eighty-five miles per hour; however, with McWilliams throwing gas, reaching the low nineties, Landry was unable to connect and went down swinging.

The Rebels had a strong lineup, top to bottom filled with high-average hitters but no one who could match Smitty's power. Instead their bread and butter was getting a guy on, having him steal, and then driving him home. Jess had it in his mind that he was not going to give them that opportunity, as he was definitely not going to throw four balls to anyone, and they were going to have to work even to connect. At the end of the third inning, the Rebels had managed one base runner who reached by way of a Texas league bloop over third base. Jess quickly erased any possibility of that runner coming around by striking out the next two hitters. He felt great but was hoping for more run support. Both Stevie and Teddy had hit balls hard in the top of the third, but they went right to the left and center fielders. By the bottom of the fourth, the Rebels were taking more and more pitches trying to tire out Jess, although he would never admit it may have been working, as he was still throwing hard but getting more and more erratic. With two outs in the bottom of the fourth, Jess allowed his first walk, and the stink of it was he had been ahead of the hitter one ball and two strikes. As is human nature, Jess did not put much thought into the next pitch, as he was just trying to let some frustration out and threw a hard one that stayed right over the plate. Tuey Rankin, an option quarterback with Division I scholarship potential, placed the fat part of the bat on the ball and hit a seeing-eye double in the gap that brought around the tying run. In a way, it was almost a relief, as the Spartans were all so tight trying to hold on to a one-run lead and not wanting to be the guy who made an error and allow an unearned run.

From that point, McWillliams and Jess matched each other pitch for pitch, with few hitters even connecting—and if so, weakly—until the top of the seventh came around and a frustrated and eager Teddy Smith stood at the plate in what he knew could possibly be his last high school at bat. Teddy was bound and determined not to swing at a bad pitch, but there was no way he was walking. Regardless he forced himself to watch the first pitch go by in order not to chase something out of the zone, and sure enough, the fastball was right down the middle. It was crystal clear that McWilliams was not about to back down to anyone, even one of the best high school hitters in the country. The adrenaline was flowing in both young men, and as a result, Teddy had the presence of mind to step out and catch his breath. This was followed by McWilliams stepping off the mound in what appeared to be gamesmanship but was, in fact, out of necessity. Finally it was time for the second pitch of the intense duel. McWilliams often looked at the batter before unleashing his heat, but he knew he had a serious challenge this time and just looked at the catcher's mitt as he went into his windup.

It seemed as if the entire stadium knew a fastball was coming, and certainly, Smitty was among those. Number 5 leaned back before leaning forward and stepping toward the pitch as he began his powerful swing. The connection was pristine, and though he was a little late on the mid-ninety-mile-an-hour laser, he got it with the fat part of the bat, and it sailed well over the right center field fence. Number 5 floated around the bases like never before. He had hit a lot of big homers in his high school career, but none bigger than this one. He felt good for Coach Jimmy, for his teammates, and his community. Like the rest of the team, he could not wait to get out in the field in the bottom of the seventh and finish off the dream season. The Spartans mustered another hit in the top of the seventh, but no more runs came across the plate, and they took the field up 2–1, needing just three outs.

Jess began to spring out to the mound but was grabbed from behind by Coach Jimmy, who looked at him and smiled and said "Just take your time, hoss. Walk out there and enjoy it. Besides I don't need you straining your damn hamstring now!"

As Jess threw his warm-up pitches, he tried to soak up the environment, as he did not know where he would be in a year. Maybe baseball was in his future, but he still felt that rodeo was his first love, and that was his most likely path. The stands were quiet as both the trailing Rebel faithful and the leading Spartan faithful knew a one-run lead could be overcome, but only three outs were needed. Jess faced down the first batter for some time before he finally threw a pitch, and it was a picture-perfect slider that raced right across the plate. In an instant, Jess threw two more just like the first pitch, and just like that, the at bat was over on three pitches. The next hitter was the Rebels leadoff hitter, Jason Bromley, who had one of the state's top averages. Bromley was a patient hitter and took a perfect strike from Jess. He swung at the second pitch, and Jess was up 0–2 in an instant. Bromley stepped out, caught his breath, and figured he was not going to get anything good to hit but had to be ready. Sure enough, Jess, tried to get Bromley to chase an outside fastball, but Bromley caught up with and fouled it off down the right field line to stay alive. Bromley again stepped out, and this seemed to annoy Jess, who was ready to shut this thing down and celebrate. Perhaps out of anger, or perhaps trying to be tricky, Jess threw a hard one inside, and Bromley meanwhile was reaching out over the plate, expecting an outside pitch, and therefore, the heater caught him square in the left hip.

It hurt like hell, but Bromley was on and relieved. The pressure cooker of an at bat was over. The tying run was now on, and Jess was definitely rattled. Jimmy considered the idea of warming up his lefty Landry to get the last two outs; however, he knew this would probably deal a bigger blow to the psyche of Jess, and he figured Jess could get two outs on willpower alone. The number 2 hitter in the Rebels lineup was Brandon Hooper, another accomplished football player from West Texas who was a pretty damn good baseball player as well. Jess knew Hooper could swing it, but red-hot Tuey Rankin was on deck.

Jess knew that he had to get Hooper, and then he could intentionally walk Rankin. (Although he was only going to do that if Coach Jimmy told him he had to!) Jess did not like taking much time between batters or pitches, and he was not going to change this now. As soon as Hooper stepped in, Jess unloaded, and it was a perfect strike right at the knees. Hooper dug in and was ready for another fastball; however, it did it him no good, as he swung and missed badly. At this point, Jess began to look over at Rankin in the on-deck circle and started to think a little bit.

Why was he thinking? Thought Jimmy. "Just throw, Jess, just throw. Concentrate on the guy at the plate!"

Jess put the ball behind his back as he began his windup from the stretch position. He fumbled the ball behind his back, between his fingers, going between a slider and a fastball grip. Ultimately Jess made the split-second decision to go with the slider and let the pitch fly. As the pitch raced toward the plate, Hooper took one step toward the plate and extended the bat with his arms. Baseball is definitely a game of inches, and the baseball gods were looking down on Hooper on this day as the screaming slider connected with the sweet spot of the TPX aluminum bat, and the ball shot toward the right center field fence. Simultaneously, center fielder Gary Looker and right fielder Brad Landry ran back toward the Dell Diamond fence in a panic. As both sides of the bleachers watched in nervous silence, the ball cleared the fence by inches and landed in the first row of the right field bleachers.

Just like that, it was over, for the seniors of Harbor Lake and their families. Meanwhile, the Midland Lee faithful were roaring, yet the Spartan players were in a daze and could hear nothing. Eventually, after what seemed like forever but was actually only a couple of minutes, Stevie began to jog in from the outfield and found Number 5, his longtime buddy, watching the Rebels celebrate from outside the Spartans dugout. The two amigos embraced, and Smitty spoke into Stevie's ear. "It was a hell of a run, Mac, a hell of a run!"

Mac managed to break into a smile and then turned toward Smitty's ear, "Sure was, brother. Now let's go waste some chickenshit Taliban!"

CHAPTER 7

The Military Entrance Processing Station, or MEPS, seemed to be the same no matter what city or state you were in. It was always a depressing old building where you could see and smell the walls leaking. Everyone who worked there was irritable, and all the recruits about to depart from there to various boot camps across the nation were always quiet and apprehensive and praying for a last-minute reprieve. Most of the recruits had spent one last night of freedom in hotel near the station and had a 5:00 a.m. wake-up call. They had no curfew their last night, and most could not sleep anyway. Therefore, the building was mainly filled with hungover, exhausted, and scared young men who wondered how they would make it through the upcoming months and even the current day. They were already being yelled at, shuffled around like cattle, and referred to either by their last name or simply as Recruit.

Stevie and Teddy were given no guarantee that they would be in the same recruit company upon arrival at the Marine Corps Recruit Depot only that they would go to the same location, San Diego, as opposed to Parris Island, South Carolina, the East Coast and older USMC Boot Camp locale. Since they shared the same recruiter, the two young men also had the luxury of sharing a hotel room their last night as opposed to rooming with someone random and were able to stay up all night watching movies and psyching each other up for the days to come. Their parents had wanted to drop them off at the MEPS at five thirty, which was an option; however, the boys wanted to get their good-byes over with the day before and check into the hotel with the recruits from more distant towns.

One thing that made this day a little easier was that there was no girlfriend to kiss farewell as Teddy had sworn off a serious girlfriend his senior year, and Stevie made a point to avoid his former dream girl, Renee, all summer. Senior enlisted staff from the local USMC recruiting depot knocked on their door at 0515 and told them they needed to be downstairs in ten minutes. They were actually shown a slight degree of respect in that their door was not slammed on, and they were not screamed at in this instance as the recruiters knew who Teddy was and respected his decision to do this. This show of respect would not last long, as within minutes they were considered as worthless as everyone else at the MEPS. They would arrive in Southern California later that night and be bused to the Marine Corps Recruit Depot, San Diego, literally right next door to the San Diego International Airport.

Immediately upon stepping foot on MCRD, they knew that worthless was a step up—they were now lower than low! The weed-out process began immediately, and the two former big men on campus were quickly one of a line of young men feeling nauseous and full of regret. Stevie felt nauseous for a different reason, as he still felt like he wanted to be here at this moment, that he needed to be here. Instead, Stevie kept wondering, *What in the world have I got my friend into?* Stevie knew Teddy should be headed to a small mountain town in Idaho to begin rookie league ball after the recent major league draft but instead was now about to walk into an unknown building and continue a day and night that showed no end in sight. Boot camp had not even started yet, and they were already exhausted and already homesick. Welcome to the Big Green Weenie!

The Marine Corps did everything in threes, and therefore, the Second Recruit Battalion was broken down into three companies: Delta, Echo, and Gulf. The promise was kept to the boys that they would leave on the same day and be in the same battalion; however, they were sent to different companies. Stevie was assigned to Delta Company, and Teddy would spend the next thirteen weeks in Gulf Company. The first few days seemed eternal. The days seemed hot, and the nights seemed cold, but the real mental game was that the recruit depot was located right next to the San Diego airport. Therefore, the recruits could both hear and see planes taking off all day and much of the night, wishing they were on them, headed home or headed anywhere but where they were. Stevie and Teddy were determined not to get depressed and both, in their own ways, tried to maintain their sense of humor in the rare moments when the drill instructors (DIs) were not watching. Some of the drill instructors followed baseball and had seen a story online about a big-time prospect passing on the major league draft to become a marine. This bought Teddy a little bit more respect at times, yet at times, it could be a curse, and he was screwed with even more than the other recruits.

Speaking of the major league draft, it was set to take place in early June, only one week after the pair arrived at MCRD. Teddy wondered from time to time if he would still get picked. If so, would that team wait for him for four years, or would the team lose his rights after one year? Maybe he was being too bigheaded, as maybe the scouts had already forgotten about him; maybe it was just the Harbor Lake faithful building him up into something he really wasn't.

Stevie knew that this wasn't the case, and he knew Teddy was the real deal. Yet Stevie was unclear on what would happen too. Teams typically lost rights to a player if they were not signed within one year of the draft, and Teddy and Stevie had committed to four years. As it happened, the recruits of Gulf Company were allowed their second phone call home seven days in. There would not be another call for a while. Unbeknownst to Teddy, it was a Saturday, and it was the first day of the 2002 Major League Draft. "What's going on, Dad?" Teddy said to Billy.

"Ah, not much. Just got off the phone with some guy from the San Diego Padres."

Teddy figured that they had just called as a courtesy to tell the Smith family that they would check on Teddy in four years.

"Guy named Ira Boyle was on the phone—old Jewish navy vet, nice guy. Anyway, he said they had just taken you in the third round."

Teddy broke into a smile, figuring his dad was just messing with him. "Dad, I'm pretty tired and really don't have my sense of humor so much today. What did he really say?"

There was an awkward silence for a minute, and Billy quickly realized that his son was tired and maybe not functioning as well as normal. Billy then spoke slowly and clearly when he said, "Teddy, I would not mess with you on this. They said they are going to see what they can work out with the Marine Corps. You were the eightieth overall pick in the country, and no one can take that away from you!"

With that, Teddy told his dad he had to go and quickly fell into ranks with his fellow Gulf Company recruits amid the screaming. However, there was a new pep in his step and a smile that would be hard to wear off his face for quite a while.

Meanwhile, over in Delta Company, Stevie knew exactly what day it was, and he was wondering who selected his buddy and if his buddy knew by now where he was drafted? Stevie snapped out of his daydreaming to screams from his senior drill instructor as Delta Company was being formed up to head to the phone center themselves. The recruits were given about five minutes apiece to call home, so they had to be prepared what to ask for and what they wanted to talk about. When J. P. McClanahan answered the phone in Harbor Lake, Stevie quickly asked, "Dad, what round did Teddy go in? Who took him, Dad?"

JP knew this question was coming and wanted to answer, but he wanted to tell Stevie he was proud first. "Hey, bud, we're all damn proud of you. You hang in there, OK?" Stevie appreciated the words but before he could respond, his dad quickly continued, "And as far as Teddy, the team down the road from you guys in San Diego took him in the third round."

Stevie got a little choked up and tried not to let his Dad know, but there was no shame in it. "Good for him!"

At that point, JP was able to tell his beloved son what he had been waiting to tell him all day. "Oh, and by the way, a guy from Chicago White Sox just called, and they picked you in the forty-seventh round." Stevie could tell by the emotion in his dad's voice that he was not lying. JP got out one more sentence before Delta Company's phone time expired, "He said the Sox thought you were a very mature guy, and I told them, 'You're damn right, he is. You're damn right, sir!'"

With that, Stevie hung up the phone and left the MCRD phone center. He too left with a pop in his step and a smile that was hard to drag away. It was great feeling knowing that someone out there (other than his dear old dad) actually believed in him! The next few weeks were a blur for the Harbor Lake boys. They were exhausted and excited at the same time, knowing that they had a memory of the MLB draft that they would never forget no matter what happened from this summer forward. The only negative vibe in both Spartans' karma right now was that they had not seen each other since the news.

Finally on 4 July 2002, with graduation a no longer impossible six weeks away, Delta Company ran into Gulf Company as one entered the chow hall and the other was exiting. Most recruits looked alike, but no one had the goofy walk of Smitty, and Stevie saw him from hundreds of feet away. He wanted to get close enough to shake his hand, but he knew he would pay the price. Fortunately the traffic congestion of bodies allowed Gulf to flow a little closer to Delta, and Stevie timed his words as perfectly as he could, "Hey, Number 5. Congrats, you bastard, congrats!"

Smitty's head popped ninety degrees at the familiar voice, and he retorted, "You too, you no-hitting son of a bitch!"

The boys knew that the drill instructors had probably heard them and they were going to get hammered when they returned to their barracks, but they did not care as they both felt, without a doubt, the exchange was worth it!

When both companies returned to their respective barracks, both recruits went through some pushups and flutter kicks and other standard punishment due to their ignoring the standing "No talking in the chow hall" rule. Neither the Gulf Company nor the Delta Company drill instructors had it in them to hammer the two friends for too long, as they were all aware of the relationship and what the two boys had passed on to be here. The DIs could never admit it, but they had respect for the boys and what they stood for, even as lowly recruits. The boys could sense that they had been treated leniently for their transgression, and both thought *Hey, maybe these drill instructors are human after all.*

Both boys had given some thought during the enlistment process to requesting artillery as their MOS and becoming 0811s (gun bunnies). However, given that Arty wasn't be used as much in the current conflict and the boys wanted to make 100 percent sure they were in the thick of it, they ultimately enlisted to become 0311s (grunts), and therefore, after graduation, they were slated to head up the road to the School of Infantry (SOI) at the massive Marine Corps Base Camp Pendleton.

First, however, there was the issue of boot camp graduation. Although time had flown, most of the recruits could not really remember what their parents looked like. Every recruit had an altered appearance somehow; most losing weight, with others adding muscle. The majority of thoughts in the week leading up to graduation were positive; however, some worried if their relationship with their girlfriend would be the same and if they were ready for life again outside the borders of the Marine Corps Recruit Depot.

All the butterflies and negative vibes went away in an instant when the respective companies walked out on the parade deck. The two dads from Harbor Lake could feel their chests expand with price as they both instantly found their sons among the pristinely marching soon-to-be marines.

Stevie's mom heard the marine officer over the loudspeaker describe her son's company as recruits and wondered aloud, "Why is he still calling them that?"

"Just hold on," said JP. "They have about three more minutes as recruits."

As it turned out, it was about ninety seconds later when the commanding officer of MCRD, Colonel Benjamin Colby, took the podium and said, "Good morning, Delta Company. Good morning, Fox Company. Good morning, Gulf Company. Good morning, *marines.*"

The entire second battalion, no longer recruits, returned a roaring, "Good morning, *sir!*"

Just like that, they had graduated to lowly privates first class and lance corporals.

CHAPTER 8

The School of Infantry at Camp Pendleton, California, just up the road seemed like paradise to the Harbor Oak two. They arrived there after ten days on leave at home, feeling like a million bucks. They loved their hometown even more than they had remembered, yet they were not depressed to leave. They had heard good things about Pendleton, a base with beautiful views, beachfront training areas, and close to San Diego and numerous other California hot spots. The pride they felt arriving home in uniform with their eagle, globe, and anchor affixed was amazing, yet they knew there was more to accomplish, more to experience, and they were ready to get it started.

When they arrived at SOI near the Camp Horno section of Camp Pendleton, fall was just staring in Southern California. The weather was perfect, and the boys had caught a break in that Pendleton could get scorching hot in the middle of July. The gents were in sister companies and had barracks right next to each other and had an entire weekend off after checking in before the training would start with a vengeance. The weekend off, the pair were floating on air as they headed into San Diego and booked a room and walked about town with cheap beer buzzes, feeling good about what they had just accomplished, earning the eagle, globe, and anchor. They sensed that girls were looking at them, and they struck up conversations pretty easily. They were in shape and confident and had nothing to lose, as if one group of girls blew them off, another was sure to be close by. They returned to SOI on Sunday and were told a 0600 formation was scheduled for Monday for day 1 of their path to becoming official 0311s, infantry marines. As the corps loves to do that was somehow changed to 0500 and the boys were in for long day!

The training was indeed physical and the days long, yet as eighteen-year-old athletes fresh out of thirteen weeks at MCRD, it just did not seem to faze the majority of recruits. There were blisters and some rashes and some irritability, but when liberty was called and you did not have duty, all the aches quickly went away. The boys would head to San Diego or sometimes Orange County, and when money was really tight, they would head to Tijuana, a.k.a. TJ. The funny thing was that Tijuana was supposed to be off-limits for marines and sailors for the most part, especially junior personnel, yet everywhere you went, all you saw were squids and jarheads. The boys were beginning to understand why everyone wanted to live in California as the beaches were clean and the women were beautiful and the weather was always nice. Too bad it was so damn expensive!

As SOI came to a close, the young marines were anxiously awaiting their duty assignments. Many would remain at Camp Pendleton, which houses the First Marine Regiment, the Fifth Marine Regiment, as well as the Eleventh and most of the Fourth. All these regiments were in need of bodies to fill their infantry battalions for the ongoing global war on terror. Down the road from Camp Pendleton, near Palm Springs, was a huge training base that now housed one battalion from the Fourth Marine Regiment as well as the entire Seventh Marine Regiment. This base was desert at its worst and had once been an army base before the army declared it uninhabitable. This place was officially called the Marine Air Ground Combat Center, Twentynine Palms. The boys of Harbor Lake were headed to the Second Battalion of the Seventh Marine Regiment, a.k.a. 2/7, located in the heart of the beautiful Mojave Desert.

The base itself was not horrible during off time, as there was a theater, gym, enlisted club, convenience store, and several fast-food establishments within walking distance. The things that made it miserable were the one-hundred-degree days in the field training, and then, come the weekend, you were literally in the middle of nowhere. Unlike most towns near military bases, the city of Twentynine Palms did not support the base at all and seemed almost offended that it was even there. The town offered absolutely nothing for marines and sailors except a Denny's. Twentynine Palms most popular occupation was methamphetamine producer, and you could forget about a Hooters or even a Chili's ever opening in town. If you wanted a decent restaurant with cute waitresses, you had to go forty-five minutes away to Palm Springs, where just about everyone was rich or gay or both. Most marines got as far away as they could on off weekends and drove through the desert to Las Vegas or went down to San Diego. The drive there was never bad, but the drive home seemed to take forever on a Sunday night as it always a painful reminder of just how remote the Twentynine Palms marines were.

With every negative, however, comes a positive, and the positive thing about the Palms was that the marines there were even tighter than the average platoon; they had to be. They were around each other so much that they knew everything about each other for better or for worse. Smitty and Stevie had both landed in Echo Company and were grateful that their goal of serving close together was actually coming true. Smitty was entrenched in Second Platoon, while Stevie rolled with jarheads of First Platoon. After spending the fall of 2002 training together day after day, week after week, the grunts were ready to go fight in the real deal. They had all thought they were headed to Afghanistan to chase Bin Laden and those cocky little Talibans; however, unbeknownst to most, another storm was forming.

The boys had some recollection of Desert Storm in 1991 and knew that the first President Bush had tangled with one Saddam Hussein. Well, now the word on the street was that the second President Bush—George W., that is—wanted to finish the deal. The training plan for 2/7 was about to be radically changed from the mountain mind-set of Afghanistan to a desert training environment in anticipation of the Persian Gulf, and what better place to train in a desertlike environment than Twentynine Palms? Nope, the leathernecks of 2/7 were not going anywhere *yet*.

There were only a few salty old dogs of 2/7 that were in the corps during Desert Storm. These hardened vets had told the young marines how much the waiting for months and months during Desert Shield had worn on them and hurt morale and caused inner strife. Thus the marines were not disappointed when they found out they would not be a part of the buildup for what would eventually become Operation Iraqi Freedom. All military branches were sending contingents to Kuwait in the winter of 2002–2003 to prepare for an eventual invasion of Iraq, with the goal of ousting Saddam Hussein from power for good. The grunts did not want to sit around at base camp for months and months, waiting to invade. Instead they wanted to get there, invade, take care of business, and get home. As the invasion date grew closer and closer, Echo Company began to worry that they might miss out on the real deal. What if it was over in a week like the ground war of Desert Storm? The marines were told that they were slated to replace their sister battalion 1/7 after the invasion inevitable took place. The spring of 2003 seemed eternal as the fighting began and the Harbor Oak boys and their buddies watched from the sidelines on CNN.

The coverage this time around was even broader and more ridiculous, as many reporters were carelessly running shoulder to shoulder with infantry and turning their backs to the enemy to face cameras. It seemed as if every unit had a reporter embedded with it, and there were live reports on just about every network on earth daily. Most of the Echo Company marines were in the weight room at the top of the hill when they saw the small corner TV playing images of Saddam Hussein's statue falling. Saddam was nowhere to be seen, and the troops began taking over palace after palace and making them their barracks across the country. Finally, in the fall of 2003, the former dictator was found, not in a plush bunker or in another nearby country being hidden away in luxury; he was found hiding in small hole in a yard with a board covering him. Filthy, exhausted, and defeated, he was taken to an undisclosed location to await trial for at least a small percentage of all the heinous crimes he had committed against his own citizens.

Well, this ground war had been longer than Desert Storm; however, it was still over quickly. There was loss of life, no doubt; however, the death count was not near as bad as feared. The fears of the troops being gassed did not come to fruition, and the word was that most of the invading troops would be coming home soon. So what did that mean for Echo Company 2/7? Would they be missing out on this fight as well? Would they now go to Afghanistan? Would they be going anywhere at all? Finally, word was passed at a formation in May 2004; they were in fact going to the Al Anbar Province in Iraq, the "Wild West." The battalion would ship out in August 2004 and would be spending Thanksgiving and Christmas, New Year's Day and Super Bowl Sunday on the sand. *Oh well*, thought Stevie, *at least the wait is over. Let's get this thing started!*

Stevie and Teddy decided not to take leave and head home as much of the battalion did in early August prior to their 23 August departure date. They did not want the drama of another in-person good-bye, and therefore, they hung out in Palm Springs and mixed in a trip to Vegas. The boys were convinced they had made the right decision when they listened to marines returning from leave who detailed painful good-byes with families and friends. The company was given one last night off on 22 August prior to a late night flight on the twenty-third scheduled to head to Ireland and then Kuwait. The group hit the pubs, and many ended up back at the hotel pool, where group singing and storytelling took place. They all passed out at some point and awoke with cotton mouth and then mounted up for the always depressing ride back to Twentynine Stumps.

CHAPTER 9

The truest saying in any branch of the military was "Hurry up and wait," and this certainly rang true for 23 August 2003 for the marines of Echo Company. They were in formation at 10:00 a.m. in the scorching Mojave Desert sun in preparation for a midnight flight leaving from nearby March Air Force Base, which would eventually stop in Ireland and then finally touch down in Kuwait. As the grunts waited in a parking lot at the bottom of a hill, the silence was eerie as the boys could not believe the on-again, off-again trip the middle to the Middle East was finally happening.

The plane left March Air Force Base and was the quietest flight any of the marines or sailors of Echo 2/7 would ever be on. The homesickness seemed to take effect immediately, and most were already thinking about the flight home, which would take place months down the line. The flight stopped in Shannon, Ireland, and the company was told they could have one beer in the small airport. As it happened, there was a unit on the way home coming through the airport and obviously, their mood was more festive. The platoon commanders of Echo quickly had to separate their personnel and make sure not only that the one-beer limit was adhered to but also that there were no fisticuffs with the homeward-bound veterans.

The brief layover was a good thing, as it snapped most of the grunts out of their depression and got them thinking about other things at least a little while. Magazines and candy were purchased, and of course, small amounts of booze were smuggled back on board. The company commander had a hunch that small bottles were purchased from the gift shop but decided not to have a shakedown. He figured he would let the boys relax for the remaining portion of the flight to Kuwait as plenty of stressful days lay ahead. There was also encouragement among the company as word spread about Camp Victory in Kuwait, where they would stop before an eventual short flight into Iraq itself. Supposedly, Victory had a Pizza Hut, a Baskin-Robbins, and a Subway. There were also nice gyms and a good free chow hall. Several young marines in the back of the charter thought aloud, "Maybe they will just keep us in Kuwait. Maybe they won't need us in Iraq."

Twentynine Palms had been consistently hot before the battalion departed, with daily temps averaging well over 100 degrees; however, Kuwait's heat made the Mojave Desert feel like Minnesota. By early morning, Kuwait was over 130 degrees, and dehydration was rampant among a high number of personnel before they even entered Iraq. The boys' pee was orange, and they struggled just walking from their platoon tents to the chow hall. They were told to go everywhere in pairs, and this rule was not broken, as not only was it hot but every tent on the compound looked alike and it was easy to get disoriented. Smitty and Stevie met daily at the Pizza Hut at Camp Victory and inhaled a pie. They would never eat pizza every day back home for fear of getting fat; however, weight gain was hardly going to be an issue working outside in three-digit heat for the next few months. They figured they would enjoy something American while they still could, and both could not help but wonder how many college students there were ordering pizzas on campuses and not giving a rat's ass about what was going on in Southwest Asia? Meanwhile there were rumors that the platoons of Echo Company were headed to different forward operating bases (FOBS) and would be split up for the remainder of the deployment. These rumors were quickly dispelled by company commander Tony Tither. The company would first be heading to Al Asad Air Base for several days, and then it was on to their new home, Camp Korean Village (KV) just outside "beautiful" Ar Rutbah, Iraq.

The flight to Al Asad from Kuwait was not pleasant as the boys roasted in the hangar for several hours before cramming on to a crowded C-130 for the hour flight to western Iraq. The week at Al Asad went quickly, and the platoons were sent by five-ton truck over to the Al Asad Airfield to load CH46 helicopters for the trip to Camp Korean Village. Once again, the silence was deafening as the boys had become accustomed to the lazy days and civilian chow of Al Asad with the Internet cafés complete with telephones. The hangar was hot, and there was no breeze on this day. The fuel and cranking engines of nearby choppers were making it even hotter. You could see the discomfort in every grunt's face as the flak jackets and helmets they were now forced to don felt like they weighed one thousand pounds. They had worn them in training; however, they had not worn them much the last two weeks, and they had felt light as a feather without the cumbersome personal protective equipment. First Platoon was on the first bird out to KV and the second and third platoons were shortly behind. When the boys landed, they were not sure what was more miserable: the heat, the noise, or the dust being kicked up by the props? Trying to laugh about the quagmire, they gathered their gear from the dirt outside the chopper and began lumbering in to the main camp. Twentynine Palms had been remote, but this small, poorly assembled camp in the far west corner of Iraq was literally the "middle of nowhere." The Echo grunts had to quickly come to grips with the fact that this shower-less, chow hall–less outpost was home for the next seven months; however, Stevie was thinking positively. *Six and three-fourths months, boys. Only six and three-fourths months!*

The turnover with the unit they were replacing would last two weeks, and as seemed to be tradition, the two weeks were quiet. It was as if the insurgents in the area were well aware a new, inexperienced unit was coming in, and they were just licking their chops. As much as American intelligence officers hated to admit it, the bad guys had intelligence too, and the bad guys seemed to always know that a combat-hardened, ingrained unit was leaving and a green unit, many of whom had never been outside the continental United States, was moving in. Therefore, the games would begin on Echo 2/7's first day flying solo throughout their sector of the area of operations. Just twenty minutes into their first mounted patrol several miles outside the wire of Camp Korean Village, the third squad of First Platoon, Echo Company went over a roadside bomb. Fortunately it was much louder than it was destructive, yet it was still scary as hell and did significant damage to the lead Hummer carrying four young grunts. The blast also did damage to the mind-sets of the First Platoon marines as their feeling of being indestructible was quickly gone.

When the First Platoon marines came back in the wire, the remainder of Echo Company could tell by the looks on their faces that this was now for real. The marines from the second and third platoons did not ask any questions other than "Is everyone OK?" The grunts from Second Platoon would be rolling out on their first patrol in the morning, and it was most definitely a sleepless night for the young warriors.

Second Platoon formed up at 0500 to head out of the gates and most were too tired to be scared. Unfortunately, the drivers were exhausted as well despite allegedly being told to bed down several hours before the rest of the platoon. Teddy loaded up in the back of a jam-packed five-ton truck that looked like it had been left to the battalion by Korean War marines. Before they even went outside the wire, they were ingesting dust galore, coughing and feeling very thirsty. It was still cool at least, since the sun had not come up yet. They all knew that the triple-digit heat was coming within a number of hours. The convoy stopped right inside the gate so that the command could be given "Go condition 1," meaning the magazine was inserted and a round was racked into the chamber. For the strong majority, this was the first time they had handled a condition 1 weapon anywhere outside of a Southern California rifle range.

The vehicles rolled down Highway 1, also known as Mobile, with some trying to sleep, some pounding water, and others just staring into space. No one knew to expect, and no one seemed to know how to relax or lighten the mood. Smitty did his best to rally his squad as he began singing old Bob Seger tunes at the top of his voice. The wind pretty much drowned him out, and most of the jarheads did not even know any classic rock-and-roll tunes anyway.

The squad was on the road about half an hour, and although they had been briefed, most did not know where they were headed, and pretty much none of them cared anyway. They were all exhausted and all fading out when they felt the vehicle slam into the guardrail, and they were all suddenly wide awake! Instantly, their training and instinct took over, and they all jumped outboard and darted away from the vehicle. They then assumed the prone position with rifles pointing toward the open desert in all directions. It was pitch-black and eerily quiet. Eventually, the adrenaline wore off, and they all just wanted to go to sleep in the prone and wake up back in California. Finally someone yelled "Clear!"—although no one really knew who. They all moved back toward their vehicles. Squad leaders began to take accountability and look for casualties.

One by one, the marines and corpsmen of Second Platoon answered when their name was shouted and reported to their squad leader. Amazingly, it appeared everyone was accounted for, and there were no serious injuries. When a total head count was taken, it was finally determined one body was missing. Just about the time the helicopters flew over, the missing body climbed out from behind the driver's seat of the impacted seven-ton truck. The driver was Eric Merritt, from Tampa, Florida, who looked more like an engineer than a marine. He was cross-assigned from the second truck battalion at Camp Lejeune, North Carolina. Merritt played for the All–Marine Corps Soccer Team and through three years had never deployed. With one year left on his contract, his number was called, and he was on his way. Merritt tried to hit the rack early the night before but could not sleep due to anxiety and as a result had fallen asleep at the wheel. The grunts were all relieved, but all wondered how many times this was bound to happen? If they are falling asleep in the back of the truck, the driver probably is too. At least it was mostly flat out here so they were unlikely to drive off a cliff!

The vehicle was determined to be serviceable, and the patrol charged on. As much as they expected to be hit, they would not see any hostile forces all day and really saw no one. It was as if the entire town of Ar Rutbah was napping or on vacation. The jarheads of Echo Company had been told by the outgoing unit that when the town was quiet or looked deserted, that was never a good sign—that it was calm before the storm. Some remembered that as the day wore on, but by about hour 16 of the day, no one even cared. All the guys were thinking was that this was still day 1, and they had a crapload of days left and a crapload of patrols to come. As their watches showed 2000 hours (8:00 p.m.), the patrol finally neared home, Camp Korean Village, and as darkness began to fall, they all could not wait to dump their gear, get their flaks off, and hit the rack. However that was not to be!

The rear vehicle in the patrol first saw what they thought was a flare fly over. The A-driver, Mark Cole, from Everett, Washington, thought *Well, this must be some type of Muslim holiday,"* and dismissed the projectile as fireworks.

Then a second object flew over their vehicle, and a third, and slowly the boys started to rub the sleep out of their eyes and look at one another. The dreaded words then came over the PRC 119 radios, "Dismount, dismount! We are under attack!" Where the hell had these chicken-shits been all day? They thought. Why can't these cowards ever attack at a decent hour?

In what was already becoming a tired tradition, the platoon assumed the prone position in a 360 and stared out at the open desert for what seemed like days. Approximately two hours later, at 2200, the order was given to mount up, and the platoon traveled the final half mile into the gates of Camp KV. The boys were told to hit the showers, but in 2004, Camp KV had no true working showers, just bottled water dumped by other marines into PCP tubes propped on the side of large general purpose tents. The shower was only slightly refreshing and way too much work after a sixteen-hour day. The boys were also hungry but too tired to even open an MRE in the dark. Even the hardiest of the platoon were a little overwhelmed at the pure exhaustion they were feeling.

Meanwhile in the Command Operations Center (COC) at Camp Korean Village, the decision had been made that four-day patrols would replace one-day patrols. This actually made good sense, as the troops would actually get more rest going out four days at a time and sleeping in the field, as opposed to driving back to the FOB every night amid the danger or darkness coupled with tired and hungry riflemen. The plan of action was passed on to the troops the next day, and squad leaders began inspecting the marines' big packs for extra T-shirts and skivvies and socks. The boys were developing rashes and blisters in daylong patrols, and therefore, the higher-ups recognized the hygiene concerns of four days at a time out in the heat with shade being a commodity.

First Platoon loaded up the following morning packed with everything they could fit, including Gatorade powder, candy (more commonly known as gee-dunk), and of course, any musical or game device that would run on batteries. The boys knew there would be downtime, and like most young Americans, they got bored easily. Of course, muster came at dark thirty—or four thirty, to be specific—with the idea they move out before light as to avoid their movements being detected. As per usual, they sat inside the gates for several hours before the order came to move just as the sun was coming up. It was already pushing one hundred degrees Fahrenheit, and as was the case every single day, it was going to get twenty to twenty-five degrees hotter by the afternoon. At least, this being the desert, the nights would be cool, so if you didn't mind the sand blowing in your teeth, you could normally get some good rack time. Everyone had to stand a two-hour fire watch though, so no night ever called for uninterrupted sleep. The platoon was dispersed into three different bivouacs around town, with one squad being set up in the city at the Iraqi National Guard (ING) headquarters for the area. The other two squads would be on the outskirts, ready to watch the highway and be ready to head into town at a moment's notice. The seldom-heard-from Third Platoon, meanwhile, would be assigned daily helicopter runs, leaving Camp Korean Village several times a day. Third would scan the area and touch down near the Jordanian and Syrian borders daily at bases such as Al Qaim. It was boring, but it meant a rack in the rear every night, and no sleeping on the ground in and around town. Little did they know that once the weather turned and the desert winter came with a vengeance, riding in a helo would become a miserable experience! There would be a massive shortage of cold-weather gear for the entire battalion, and this encompassed all ranks. Everyone had dreaded the heat and the sand, yet no one—absolutely no one—had warned the incoming battalion about the desert winter, and none of the officers had done proper research. If they had, in fact, done research and knew that Al Anbar would become so cold, they failed to pass the word on to the troops, and that was even more shameful.

Just about the time the weather was quickly going from extremely hot to briefly comfortable to bitter cold, Second Platoon was receiving word that they were being detached to Al Asad Airbase due to a request for platoon-level support from the commander of the Seventh Regimental Combat Team, currently in charge of the area of operation, known as AO Denver. At first, the hard chargers of Second Platoon could only think about the chow halls and the weight room and the Internet cafés at Al Asad. Slowly but surely, they started to realize that they probably were not being sent to Al Asad to guard the base or hang out in the rear. More than likely, they realized that they had to be going there for a more difficult and important mission. What would that mission be? When would they find out?

CHAPTER 10

The grunts of Second Platoon were given one night to pack and were on their way the next morning. They figured that they were having to truck it in a convoy but actually were transported via helicopter and arrived in time to enjoy lunch at the Halliburton-run chow hall. The first few days were exactly what they had hoped for, as they included a lot of rack time, working out, three wonderful meals a day, and no responsibility. It was as if no one knew they were there and they were getting paid to do nothing. Three days after beginning their latest Al Asad stay, the platoon was gathered and told they were going on a nighttime mission.

The butterflies built and built as the troops loaded up their vehicles in the cool desert air as the boys were anxious to get into the fight. The wind began to kick up from time to time, and no one from Second Platoon had a shred of cold-weather gear, but everyone was too amped up to care at the moment. The boys were not told much other than that they would be providing security for an element of the Third Recon Division who would be conducting raids in the town of Haditha. The platoon moved out shortly after 11:00 p.m. local time and was on the road for several hours. For once, no one slept, as they all seemed to sense their first true significant action was likely forthcoming. Eventually, the platoon arrived at a hilltop with a scenic view of the town and was told to stand fast; they would be called upon when needed and that they more than likely "would be needed!"

The boys had no idea whether or not their number would be called, and while some relaxed, others stood on edge with all their gear on, refusing to get comfortable, as if the call on the radio were to come at any minute. The Third Recon vehicles rolled down the hill with precision and perfect turns, acting as if they had done this before. The roads were generally bad all over Iraq, and when one encountered occasional hills, the roads became worse. Therefore, while the drivers had to be safe, they also could not coast into town as to provide too much warning that they were coming for an unwelcome visit.

As Recon moved in, it was quickly evident that this would be no boring patrol. Immediately, suspicious characters ran inside and took firing positions, and soon the fireworks erupted. It did not appear that anyone was hitting anything for at least five minutes until the second platoon grunts noticed a vehicle on fire. It took a moment for the boys to determine what type of vehicle it was and whether or not it was American or it belonged to local resistance or just an innocent resident. With scopes, they soon figured out that an American Hummer was ablaze, and it was unclear if there were marines inside. That question was quickly answered as Second Platoon could make out marines running toward the vehicle! They would find out later that the recon marines were running back for weapons and gear they wanted to rescue. Approximately thirty quiet minutes later, the marines headed back to the rally point and met up with Second Platoon. The mission had gone extremely well with no US casualties. Two apparent enemy fighters were killed in action (KIA), and recon brought back six suspicious military-aged adults for interrogation. Once everyone was accounted for, the convoy began heading back for Al Asad. It had been a short night, a successful night; however, most of Second Platoon was upset that they had missed out on the action themselves.

Meanwhile, back at exotic Camp Korean Village, Stevie and First Platoon were beginning their routine of heading outside the wire for four days at a time and bedding down on the ground, under the stars, outside of town, and near the major roads. The days were long and hot yet quiet, and the time in the rear was initially pretty relaxed, with time to work out and get to the Internet. The officers at Camp Korean Village quickly came to the conclusion that the troops had too much downtime during their four days in the rear, and this was going to lead to fights and preventable accidents. In addition, the officers knew that despite their best efforts, alcohol was being mailed in to the camp every day. The leadership quickly came up with the idea to approach the regimental combat commander with the proposal of daily helo missions for the troops to overlook the borders. Border forts were supposedly going up along both the Jordanian and Syrian borders. It was proposed that First Platoon would fly overhead daily to make sure the locals contracted to build these forts were actually doing their jobs and that the forts were not being booby-trapped. This seemed logical in that they could prevent sabotage at least while they were overhead; however, could they have realistically found a way to keep eyes on these forts twenty-four hours a day? To the enlisted marines, this certainly seemed like busy work.

The time was indeed moving quickly as they were told that it would, and next thing the boys knew, it was late October. Both in Al Asad and near Camp Korean Village, the weather was turning cooler at night, yet once again, no one seemed to have any clue of how cold the Iraqi desert could get. First Platoon got their initial taste on their inaugural helo mission at 0600 on 8 October 2004, as they formed up in the darkness and realized they were all shivering. They were all muttering to themselves and then aloud, "Come on, you freaking sun, hurry up and rise already!"

In early October, Camp Korean Village still had no real chow hall, although they did seem to have a growing dog population. Stray dogs would infiltrate the camp daily, and the marines could not believe how cute some of the desert dogs were. Officially none of the dogs could be kept in tents for sanitation reasons, and this was a good rule. However with homesickness running rampant, certain marines were secretly adopting certain dogs, and the pooches were picking up on this, knowing where to go for food and when.

At Al Asad, Smitty did not look at pictures from home and tried to block out images of his family's faces. Wanting to stay zoned in on the job he had to do, he was able to block out these images for the most part, yet he just could not block out the smiling face of his beloved pooch, Sandy. Oddly, the first thing he wanted to do when he got home was take his pooch for a walk around Harbor Lake. Eventually Smitty took to carrying a picture of his pooch in his left breast pocket. While others would take out pictures of their girlfriend or their wife, the young slugger would stare over and over at a photo of his loyal four-legged buddy. Smitty was in his rack, staring at his pooch, about to pull out his iPod when word came through the tent. "Pack up, were heading to Hit to support 2/8 [Second Battalion, Eighth Marines]. We should be back by nightfall."

The platoon moved out with Halliburton "hot plates" in tow meaning they were able to get to-go food from the civilian chow hall. A little afternoon stroll up to the Euphrates River for the day and then they could come back and eat again. The drive was quiet and uneventful for the first hour; however, as they closed in on the city of Hit right on the west side of the river, the boys heard explosions galore. The sound was deafening, and they could see projectiles of all kinds heading every direction. This was it; they finally found a firefight. But what did they do now? Smitty felt tightness in his stomach and wondered if he was the only one a little scared. He took a quick look around the back of his vehicle, which had six jarheads on benches. He could tell by the look in all their eyes that anxiety was prevalent. More than anything though, they all seemed to be shielding their ears from the noise of the projectiles impacting. Were they really only going to be at this position for the afternoon? That looked more and more doubtful by the minute.

Upon arriving at the outskirts of town the noise had become deafening. The platoon had been given a predefined area to disembark the vehicles, but that was quickly reassessed. The platoon quickly disembarked behind some buildings on the main road entering Hit on the West Side of the river. There was a shouting of orders from all directions; however, no one could hear anything. Quickly, Sergeant Vega, the platoon sergeant, began pointing and signaling with his arms where he wanted his marines to move. The mortars were impacting almost nonstop, and the impact seemed to be getting closer and closer.

"I thought these bastards couldn't aim," said Smitty aloud, although no one could hear him. Maybe the rumors were not true. Maybe they were not all horrible marksmen with mortars or small arms. The platoon moved in and out of one-story buildings down the road toward the river and quickly deciphered that the town had been abandoned. With the platoon commander hanging back in a vehicle, this ground patrol was Sergeant Vega's, and he had to make an instant decision as to where to go. Vega was quickly able to decipher that the town was abandoned and that all the houses were empty. He called the squad leaders up, and each squad was instructed to take their fire teams to one of three houses on a perpendicular road facing the river.

Smitty's fire team, led by Sergeant Aaron Early, quickly broke through a door of the third house down and made sure the house was clear. The team was surprised by how many rooms there were in the house, how well the rooms were furnished, and how clean the house was in general—weird things to be thinking about with all the noise and confusion and adrenaline. Of course, the first thing Smitty thought was that "this was nice house, and it had to have plumbing, right?" Well, as was the case with 99 percent of the houses in Al Anbar, the house had everything other than running water. This house even had a satellite dish with a good-sized television that had Arabic and even some English channels. When Sergeant Early, a clean-cut kid from the LA suburbs, realized that his team was checking out the accommodations, he quickly told them not so subtly to get back on track and move to the roof. This was not a hotel room. This was nothing short of a large bunker!

When the team made it to the roof they were surprised again how the flat roof was decorated and thought it looked a lot like a wealthy person's home in Southern California that could be used for sunbathing. The boys were even more taken aback by the sheer amount of smoke and destruction they picked up in their panoramic view on both sides of the river. The next hour was spent in the prone position just listening to the firing in every direction and hoping the next mortar that impacted did not hit the house they were in!

Before they knew it, the sun was setting, and the platoon would definitely be spending an unplanned night outside the city of Hit. The rooftops were getting cold, and the marines had no cold-weather gear. They also had virtually no food and no water. As the firing began to settle down, a duty rotation was set up, which called for two marines staying awake at a time.

As he lay down and tried to sleep prior to his rotation on watch in two short hours, Smitty began wondering how the Houston Astros were doing in the play-offs and if they were going to be eliminated again by their longtime nemesis, the Atlanta Braves? He knew he should not be thinking about baseball at a time like this, but he was wishing at this very moment that he was home watching the play-offs with his dad. Roy Oswalt was the ace for the Astros, and when the boys left Al Asad, they knew from the Internet that Oswalt was taking the mound in a decisive game 5 of the first round of the play-offs. Up until 2004, the Astros had never won a play-off series, and more often than not, it was the Braves that knocked them out. As he lay on the concrete roof, using a poncho liner for warmth, he was trying to avoid thinking about the hunger pangs and the thirst overcoming him. He soon began feeling sad for the many Iraqis, especially the children, who must feel hunger pangs regularly during this war, and the thousands who had been displaced from their homes, never knowing when or if they could return.

Back at Camp Korean Village, First Platoon was not minding so much their rotation of heading outside the wire four days at a time. There were fewer officers, plenty of books. Candy, iPods, and open spaces seemed to calm the young marines. There was the occasional cold mounted patrol into the city and, sometimes, late-night foot patrols and raids on houses in Ar Rutbah, yet much of the time was sent on overwatch posts looking down at the town and watching the sunsets.

Stevie obviously had time to think, and he wondered what Smitty was doing over at Hotel Al Asad. Little did Smitty's old friend know that he was on a rooftop near the Euphrates River merely hundreds of yards away from numerous insurgents who wanted to kill him and all his buddies.

Two hours came and went in an instant as Smitty passed out hard, not realizing how exhausted he truly was. When he awoke, there were still intermittent explosions, and he was amazed how immune he had already become to the noise. Smoke filled the air, and the wind seemed to be blowing the smell of trash and gunpowder directly on their rooftop. The good news is that an element of marines that Second Platoon was replacing left them a seven-ton full of water bottles and meals ready to eat, and the food and water was being distributed among the houses that they occupied. The bad news was that the boys still had no clean socks, no clean shirts or underwear, and no deodorant or toothpaste. Smitty did not really care so much about any of that (although dry socks always sounded good). What he really longed for was a nice big swish of mouthwash.

While the situation on the rooftops was mildly uncomfortable, it was about to take a big turn to the south, and the boys would soon end up missing their perches atop the roofs. Within several hours, word came in that the platoon needed to move to a palm grove with a better view of the river. Again, the boys figured a few hours of looking at the river and they would be headed back to Al Asad for huge helpings of civilian chow. When the boys overheard Lieutenant Kindorf, the platoon commander, discussing a plan to raid the local shops for toothpaste, they all realized they would not be leaving anytime soon.

Sure enough, Corporal Jerry Boerstler, a stocky but fit former fullback, was leading a fire team to the rear of the palm grove in search of hygiene items. While Boerstler and his team were in route toward town, the mortars again began to come inbound, and the platoon had to dig into the palm grove using whatever they could for cover. Although the noise was deafening, the platoon was not bothered much by the blasts impacting to their rear as they were much more worried about their missing fire team.

Almost on cue, the mortars stopped, perhaps for prayer break, and Boerstler's team came strolling back into the palm grove with goodies. The mission had been accomplished as they returned with more than an ample supply: foot powder, candy, and some type of funky lotion that felt good on the skin nonetheless. Deodorant was almost impossible to find in this country, but fortunately for Smitty, they were able to find toothpaste, and he was able to finally get the funky taste out of his mouth and go on to worrying about other issues.

CHAPTER 11

Back home in Harbor Lake, Texas, the boys' parents had become accustomed to regular e-mails from their marines, which at least, to a degree, helped the time pass faster. The good news was that the families rarely went more than four days without hearing from their beloved offspring. The bad news was that in the Internet generation, it was instantly known when there was an explosion in Al Anbar and that there were casualties.

As day 3 turned into day 4 of what was to be a four-day mission, Smitty was wishing he could e-mail his parents or someone back home. Obviously, he wanted to know how they were doing, but despite being dirty, hungry, exhausted, and somewhat scared, he really wanted to know if the Houston Astros had finally made it out of the first round of the play-offs! He once again reminded himself that he should not be thinking about something so trivial at a time like this, yet he knew that it was also relaxing him and helping him stay focused. The loud booms quickly interrupted his thought of the MLB Playoffs as, once again, mortars were flying over the river. The mortars were soon followed by tracers and machine gun fire. The platoon had a good hiding place, yet it was apparently not good enough!

After an eerie period of calm, the fire started coming in with more and more of a vengeance. Tree branches started falling, and the rounds seemed to be impacting earlier and earlier. Lieutenant Kindorf soon sent out the order for every marine and sailor to grab his entrenching tool. They were definitely not moving for a while, and they needed to dig fighting holes as deep as they could. The good news for Smitty was that he was paired with Beau Wimberly, the easternmost marine in the entire company. Wimberly hailed from Shrewsbury, Massachusetts, and could handle a shovel like no one else! Before Smitty knew it, he had a fighting hole nearly three feet deep and almost five feet long. Not only did he feel safer, but getting down in the foxhole also provided tremendous shelter from the wind as the temperature continued to drop with every day the boys remained in Hit.

Of course, instead of giving Beau a straight compliment, Smitty had to give him a backward compliment as per USMC style. "You're going to be one hell of a ditch digger when you get out of the corps, son, one hell of a ditch digger!"

Back at Korean Village, Stevie had some down time after a helicopter mission to the border and waited for his thirty minutes allowed on a computer. Once online, Stevie expected to have some e-mails waiting from his buddy Smitty. Both friends only communicated with each other and their families as time and energy did not really allow for staying in touch with many other people. Stevie knew they were like a couple of teenage girls sending text messages, but he did not care. They picked each other up when one was down, and the communication also helped make the deployment go by so much faster. At first Stevie was just disappointed that he had no message from his buddy; however, when he checked again the next day, his disappointment turned to concern.

Like most others, Smitty did not have any idea that Western Iraq was freezing in the winter, and he was wondering why every night in Hit seemed to get colder. As they lay on the wet, dirty ground, he alternated thinking about how he would like a warm shower and how nice a clean pair of socks would be. Ironically, Smitty had constantly gotten on to younger guys about attention to detail including always packing an extra pair of socks, yet he himself had no socks, and his feet were rank, with a new blister forming almost daily. The corpsmen were doing what they could for the blisters, draining them and distributing moleskin. Cream was being handed out for the various other rashes. The boys all needed some good news, as tension was high and morale was low. Not a moment too soon, there was a mental break, at least for Smitty, from the now four-day patrol that was supposed to be a couple of hours.

Jared Rodgers, a lanky baseball lover from the Chicago suburbs was given permission to use the platoon commander's satellite phone. Rodgers had legitimately called home to check on his ailing father but had also inquired about the goings-on in the sports world. As soon as Rodgers hung up the phone, he made his way to Smitty's foxhole and gave the young slugger the news he wanted to hear. "Hey, man, Oswalt pitched a gem, the Astros finally made it out of the first round."

Once again, Smitty knew he had his priorities in the wrong place but did not care. The Astros were moving on Saint Louis, and he seemed more excited about that than perhaps eventually making it out of the city of Hit.

As the sun came up on day 5 of their "afternoon patrol," the marines of Second Platoon could sense the explosions getting farther and farther away. Although no one wanted to say it aloud, there seemed to be a common feeling that they may be heading back to Al Asad in the very near future. Showers definitely sounded like an appealing undertaking for every marine and corpsman of the platoon; however, food sounded even better. MREs were still in good supply, but no one could eat them anymore. They were all constipated and thirsty and dirty and just flat irritable. Most of the older marines, and perhaps some of the younger ones, knew that many a field patrol in Vietnam and Korea and WWII and Desert Storm and even the invasion of Iraq had gone longer than five days, yet they didn't care. They respected those grunts for what they went through but, at this point, felt there was nothing to prove. They were hardened enough, they wanted showers and to catch their breath, and then they would move on the next operation. They were tired of looking at Hit, the Euphrates River, and the guy next to them. They needed different surroundings; either that or they needed a real target to shoot at instead of a quiet river and abandoned houses.

Meanwhile over at Shangri-La, the boys of First Platoon were fired up that the army reserve had moved into the camp and put up real shower tents. The boys had been using bottled water for their entire tour to date, and with the weather turning colder by the day, hot water was a gift from above. The camp was also due for its first celebrity visit, as comedian Colin Quinn was scheduled to be making a visit prior to Thanksgiving. As it turned out, the boys were tasked with a mission that night and did not get to see the show, complete with mini steaks in the warm chow hall. Of course, the steaks were like leather, but steaks nonetheless, and the chow hall on KV had heat, unlike the roads outside Ar Rutbah.

Just as Stevie's thoughts were turning away from baseball and toward chips and *queso* and margaritas, he suddenly felt the earth around him move. He initially figured it was just a seven-ton truck dropping off more marines from another company. Shortly thereafter, he heard the booms and realized along with his platoon mates that the mortars were coming again, and this time they were even closer. The entire platoon had been leaning against a house, eating MREs, and quickly had to scramble for their gear and look for a more secure position. They had houses behind them if the mortars fell short, but in front of them was just open road, and if a mortar landed there, the shrapnel would be headed right for them. Kindorf quickly gave the order for all hands to dart back into the palm grove, closer to the river. The boys were in for another night sleeping in the dirt, and warm chow and showers would have to wait yet another day.

CHAPTER 12

Fifteen October 2004, started out as a humid day, yet to the group of Southern boys among Second Platoon, it felt just like waking up for a day of tailgating. The lingering smells of gunpowder coupled with the wind blowing it in their direction made it seem even more humid. There was trash everywhere, and they were all developing one type of rash or another.

Hospital Corpsman Second Class Johnnie Martin was running low on creams, powder, and anything of the like he could hand out for hygiene purposes. The hard-charging corpsman had plenty of medical gear at all times, which made for a heavy assault pack; however, he was not anticipating any preventative medicine being needed on a four-hour mission. Martin was as country as it gets, from a small town in South Carolina, and loved any and all types of weapons. Despite the fact he was only supposed to fire his weapon when his patient was in danger, he carried a full combat load of six magazines plus several more in his cargo pockets. In addition to his M16, Martin had an M9 pistol with several loaded magazines and a giant Ka-Bar knife. The guys poked fun at him but had to be impressed with his medical knowledge; he learned on the fly but remembered everything. He was a walking *Physicians' Desk Reference*, with an amazing knowledge of pharmacology. Johnnie was also good at predicting things and fashioned himself somewhat of a psychic. Although he seemed to spew a lot of nonsense, more often than not, what he sensed actually came to be.

For this reason, the grunts of Second Platoon were none too pleased when Martin said, "We're going to get hit one more time before they leave this town." The jarheads all stared at him with looks of disgust yet knew it was a good reminder to the platoon not to let their guard down. Although no one had been seriously hurt up to this point, they all had brass burns from their own rounds firing off, blisters, and rashes and scrapes galore. All of those were just annoyances; the platoon wanted to get away from the river with no lost limbs and definitely without losing any marines!

Shortly thereafter, the shouts were heard from all directions, "Load up!" and "We're moving out!" Was this just another tease? Were they really heading out of town back to Showerville and the land of hot chow, or was it just another tease? No more than thirty seconds after the last body was loaded up in the Hummers and five-ton trucks, the first impact was heard and felt. The first mortar round knocked everyone down in the bed of the trucks and those in the Hummers hit their heads against the roof and doors; fortunately, everyone had their Kevlar helmet, and no one actually fell out of a vehicle. The next mortar seemed a great deal louder and definitely closer. Without the order even being given, the marines quickly dismounted the vehicles and ran to the outside wall of the closest building and assumed a crouched position. The thing that sucked was you had no idea if the next round might hit the very building you were using for cover.

Once again, the communication had to become instantaneously nonverbal, as the noise was deafening. In addition, the ground was shaking with every impact, and guys were losing their balance as they tried to move and become more and more spread out. They eventually were able to get accountability for all forty-two marines and sailors, and amazingly, once again no one had a scratch.

It was at this point that Lieutenant Kindorf had to make another extremely difficult decision. Knowing that his marines were tired, filthy, and barely combat-ready, he desperately wanted to get to the rear, if even for a day! They were out of MRES, extremely low on water, and low on ammo, and there was no guarantee that a resupply was coming anytime soon. Kindorf began to grab the radio and call the other vehicles for his squad leaders' input, but quickly aborted that plan. He proceeded to run to them one by one so that he could hear it from them without knowing what the others felt—did they want to move, or did they want to stay? All three squad leaders and his platoon sergeant were quizzed, and they all told the young lieutenant in no uncertain terms that time, "It is time to get out of this dirty town for good!"

With that, Kindorf ran to his vehicle and made the transmission to the rear element, "This is Echo 2/6. We are moving out. Seven victors, forty-two packs."

The A-driver in each vehicle heard the transmission and nodded to the driver that it was time to hit the gas. The marines in the seven-tons all exhaled, as this time they were actually moving. Smitty was in the last seven-ton truck on the left bench closest to the tailgate. As the wheels began to turn, a fellow marine's rifle slipped from his grasp and began to fly out of the rear of the truck, over the tailgate and into the dust. At that precise moment, Smitty stood up from the bench and reached to grab the airborne weapon. At the same moment, the last mortar from across the river impacted behind the rear vehicle, and sent shrapnel in every direction. All of the marines in the back of the vehicle fell to the deck, and miraculously, the shrapnel missed and went over and around all of them—all of them except one!

The first thing that bothered Smitty was the incredible amount of dust. He was inhaling windblown dust by the gallon, it seemed. His uniform was covered in an inch plus layer from head to toe, and he could not see a foot in front of him in any direction. Shortly thereafter, Smitty noticed a lake of dust flowing around in him, which was dust mixed with some type of liquid. Time was a blur; however, he eventually discerned that the liquid causing the "dust lake" around him was red. Was it blood? He wondered. *Whose blood is it? Is someone hit?* The fit young Texan then attempted to get up on his feet. He began to try to push off the ground with his left hand in order to go and help whichever marine may be down, at that point, the adrenaline finally began to slow down, and Number 5 noticed that the "blood lake" was from his own left hand as well as his own left foot, and he also quickly realized that the bleeding was not stopping!

Lieutenant Kindorf quickly began to make out one of his marines lying on the ground at the rear of the formation. As Kindorf moved closer, he could soon tell that it was the former high school baseball star, whom the guys jokingly called Slugger. The lieutenant then noticed how dazed his young marine was and that the marine was staring aimlessly at the blood streaming profusely out of his left hand.

As Kindorf tried to gather himself and find his radioman to call in the medevac, he noticed that there were also large amounts of blood coming from Smitty's lower left leg. The platoon commander tried not to look at the leg and alarm his marine further, yet the young devil dog picked up on the vibe and turned his eyes toward his leg. Kindorf could almost feel the heartbreak taking control of the marine's body and wanted to hold him but knew he had to get help on the way. As the lieutenant slowly took his arms off the marine, Doc Martin arrived, breathing heavily. Martin would never be accused of not packing enough medical gear, as his giant med bag was stuffed with all types of bandages, medication, and most importantly, tourniquets. As Kindorf ran to his headset, most of his marines and his gunners on the top of all his vehicles had not waited for permission to fire. They were letting rounds go across the river as quickly as their big guns would let them. Simultaneously, Weapons Company 2/7 located half a kilometer behind Second Platoon, Echo, began launching everything they had.

Despite the incredible noise and confusion, Doc Martin was remarkably calm. He laid Smitty down in a supine position and straightened out his limbs and immediately began a blood sweep from head to toe. It was impossible to miss the blood coming from his hand, and thus, Martin applied one of the CAT tourniquets around Smitty's left hand to stop the bleeding. Tourniquets had come along way fortunately, and the CAT was easy to apply and very effective. Martin continued his blood sweep down the body, both sides back and front, and saw no other wounds until the gushing red coming from Number 5's lower left leg. Martin cut the slugger's trousers to make sure he could pinpoint the wound. When he got the pants open, he saw an open fracture, meaning the bone was visible. The leg needed to be set; however, Martin knew that would have to wait. He applied a second tourniquet to the upper portion of Smitty's leg, and once again, the tourniquet was doing what it was designed to do and the flow of blood was stopping. Martin knew a dust-off helicopter would be landing soon and that they were going to have to move Smitty to a Hummer and drive him the short distance to the landing zone. Martin reached into his bag and pulled out a syrette of morphine; he could see the pain in Smitty's face as well as the depression, and he wanted to give him some comfort. He stabbed the Syrette into Smitty's right thigh and one again could see it doing what it was designed to do, which was alleviate the pain. Martin looked to the sky and pointed. *So far, so good. Lord, please let me help him live.* Two marines quickly appeared with a litter, and in the dust and confusion, Martin could not even tell who they were. Smitty was rolled onto the litter, and they picked him up and began moving him to the designated Hummer. They should have used the straps to secure Number 5 to the litter but in the rush did not do so.

As they moved toward the vehicle, Martin realized that he was not strapped, and he screamed upon deaf ears, "Don't drop him! Jesus, don't drop him!"

As he began to slide off the stretcher, Smitty used what little strength he had left and grabbed one of the marines with his good arm and managed to keep from falling off.

The rear stretcher bearer then yelled to the marine in front, "Straps! We need straps!"

CHAPTER 13

Out west at Camp KV, word was trickling in about Second Platoon being involved in the Battle of Hit, as it was being called. The word was that while they were not as involved as 2/8 or some of the other units, they definitely got some trigger time in.

Stevie questioned the officers innocently regarding whether or not Second Platoon took any casualties. He was abruptly told that there was only one known marine seriously wounded. Stevie shrugged and walked away thinking, *well, that's not bad, could have been a whole lot worse.* Stevie had no idea that the seriously wounded marine was his longtime friend and teammate.

One thing about a combat zone is that the rivalries between the different branches went largely out the window. The medical evacuation (medevac) team designated for the area of operation Second Platoon was in was made up of a mixture of US Army and US Air Force personnel. They may not do anything but play cards and shoot hoops for a day or two at a time, but when a call came in, they were all business, and they were damn good at their jobs. Within ten minutes from being relayed the call from Lieutenant Kindorf, the team, ironically coined the Lone Star Dust-Off, was nearing a predesignated landing zone (LZ) near the city of Hit. At this point, Smitty was fading in and out of consciousness, and although incredible noise spewed all around him, he heard nothing and seemed to be feeling no pain.

A decision was made by the receiving medical officer to bring Smitty to Al Asad first and then likely to a more advanced hospital in Baghdad. It was a quiet day at Charlie Surgical on Al Asad, and this was a good thing for Number 5 as he immediately received maximum attention upon landing. The attending doctors, nurses, and senior hospital corpsmen were impressed by the work that Doc Martin had done in the field. Martin had most likely prevented Smitty from dying from hemorrhaging blood from his hand and lower leg or, as it is more commonly referred to, bleeding out. In addition, Martin had completed a combat casualty card with his Sharpie that clearly identified where this marine's wounds were and what treatment he had administered to include the time the morphine was administered and the tourniquets were put in place. When Martin watched the chopper leave the outskirts of Hit, he felt good about his buddy's chances to survive; however, he immediately started thinking about Smitty's chance to play ball again. Like everyone else, he knew Smitty was a hell of a player and what the game meant to him.

Stevie did not know what to think when summoned to the office of the acting first platoon commander, Gunny Coleman, at Camp KV. What had he done? Whom had he pissed off? Was he being demoted, perhaps transferred to another platoon? Maybe it was something at home. Was something wrong at home? Maybe it was something positive. Maybe he was being promoted or at least recognized for his efforts in the platoon. His anxiety definitely rose when he walked into the small office/bedroom inside a hollow concrete building and saw the company commander, Major Horton, sitting beside Gunny Coleman! Stevie took a deep breath and slowly sank into the chair provided for him after being told he could do so.

The conversation took a relaxed tone from the beginning as Major Horton stated, "How are you holding up, devil dog? Are you enjoying your Iraqi vacation?"

Stevie relaxed a little bit as he could immediately sense that he was not about to reprimanded for something. He then responded, "Having a great time, but all good things must come to an end, don't they sir?"

"Indeed they do, Corporal. Indeed they do!"

The three men then nodded at one another, and there was an awkward silence as they all flashed half-nervous smiles. Gunny Coleman broke the silence by asking the obvious. "So you and ol' Smitty are pretty tight?"

Stevie was once again caught off guard, immediately thinking, *what had Smitty done now?* Maybe it was minor. Maybe they were just messing with him. Maybe he had stolen a bunch of desserts from the chow hall or pushed over another marine while the grunt was in the port-a-can? Stevie knew he had to finally answer the question, so he reluctantly stated, "Well, yes, Gunny, we have known each other a long time and been through a lot together."

Major Horton then chimed in, "He wanted us to talk to you before we talked to anyone else outside his platoon."

The suspense was now killing him. What had that knucklehead gotten involved in? It was then that Gunny Coleman caught him off guard.

"Second Platoon caught some hell over in Hit, and from the sound of it, Smitty got the worst of it."

Stevie knew exactly what that meant and wanted to be with his friend immediately. He then had shivers rush through him as he began to imagine where he was hit and to what extent. "How bad is he, Gunny? Where was he hit?"

"He was wounded in his foot and his hand," Gunny Coleman replied. "He is going to live, but the use of that foot and that hand are not guaranteed."

Stevie was relieved briefly but then thought aloud, "What about baseball? Can he still play ball?"

In the coming days, Charlie Surgical became more and more crowded from the crazy operational tempo of the marines in the field during the month of October. Daily conferences were now necessary among the staff, as decisions needed to be made as to what patients could be moved and how quickly. As another conference began in a makeshift conference room that was nothing more than an old storage closet, the first name that was mentioned was "Smith, Theodore. Corporal, USMC, Second Battalion, Seventh Marines."

The staff had already taken a likening to Corporal Smith, and all agreed he would be nice to keep around. However, he was stable enough to be moved by helicopter to an echelon farther in the rear where he received more advanced care and more constant attention.

In addition, Charlie Surgical had other marines and sailors, soldiers, and airmen who were in no condition to move, and they knew that others would be coming in from the field almost on a daily basis. Therefore, it was agreed upon on 18 October 2004 that on 19 October 2004, Corporal Theodore Smith would be taking a little trip to a busy facility he had heard about, the Air Force Theater Hospital at Balad Air Base, Iraq.

CHAPTER 14

Billy and his intensely faithful wife, Connie, were not immediately made aware that their son was being moved due to security risk of any movement in a combat zone. On 21 October 2004, Billy answered the phone and froze. A polite female officer, an Australian American Naval Academy grad named Kylee Stern, was on the other line. Once she identified herself, Billy wasn't nervous, yet was confused. *Why does this officer sound Australian?* He thought. Before First Lieutenant Stern could pass on any information to Teddy's dad, she had to confirm her identity. Kylee explained to Billy that she was, in fact, born in Australia; however, she had moved to Chicago at the age of ten and subsequently attended the United States Naval Academy in Annapolis.

Billy was sure that the Australian lieutenant had some news about his son; however, he was somewhat relaxed, knowing that if Teddy had passed away, there would be a chaplain and another officer or senior enlisted man standing in the Smith's living room. Still though, he was somewhat uneasy, with the thought in the back of his mind that perhaps his beloved boy's luck had taken a turn for the worse.

"Your son has begun his voyage home, sir," she began to explain.

"What does that mean?" replied Billy. "Is he in Germany?"

"No, sir, I can tell you that he has been in the rear, away from any forward operating bases."

He received a stern look from Connie as if to say "The girl would tell you everything if she could, but she is only passing along the information that she was given authorization to do." He took a deep breath and realized some information was better than none, before apologizing to the nervous lieutenant and stating, "Just tell me, when he will be stateside? When can we have him home?"

Lieutenant Stern knew this question was coming and wished she could give the brave marine's family more information and more of a timeline; however, it was impossible to do so. "All I can tell you, sir, is that we will have him safe and secure at Ramstein Air Base in Germany in the near future."

Billy wanted to lash out as he began to say "You mean to tell me that he is not safe and sound now?" He caught himself, though, and thanked her for the information. "When will I hear from you again? When will we know more?"

"Sir, I will contact you again as soon as I have an update in regard to your son. Our goal is to set up a video Skype conference for you so that you can see him, and we would likely arrange to get you overseas to Ramstein Air Base to visit him if you would like."

Billy began to perk up, and his disappointment from the lack of specific information faded. If Teddy can talk to us through video, he must not be doing so badly. He could not wait to see hear his son's voice, to see his face, to tell him how much he loved him. "Thank God for technology, Connie." He looked to his wife. "Thank God!"

As Corporal Stephen McClanahan departed the wire from Korean Village in his convoy, he was in a daze. He felt almost drunk; he was apathetic for the first time and not in a good mind-set to lead a squad of marines, or even himself, into any dangerous situation. Almost immediately after the convoy exited the gates of Camp Korean Village, Stevie was forcefully brought back into focus as fifty-caliber rounds were flying right over their vehicles from every direction. The bursts were loud, and it was not immediately clear where they were coming from. The convoy kept moving toward Highway 1, which would take them to town and safe cover, yet as they traveled, they quickly realized that they were being attacked from vehicles on the highway itself, and they were headed right into the field of fire. The good news was the small arms and machine gun fire was not accompanied by an improvised explosive device, at least not yet anyway. The order was subsequently given: disembark the vehicles, spread out, form a wedge in the prone position, and prepare for a long day.

Inside the wire, they were very aware that a platoon was under attack, and they were also able to pinpoint an area of the highway approximately just over a kilometer away. The problem was that the insurgents had stopped all traffic; the exact vehicles from which the firing was coming could not be known for sure. A counter mortar attack could be easily launched and be effective if not for the issue that had become far too common—the fear of collateral damage and the high probability of civilian casualties. Therefore, it was agreed upon by the command element inside the wire and the platoon outside the gates that the safest (at least politically) alternative available was to take cover until the insurgents either run out of ammunition or get bored. Frustrating as hell and scary as well—as a well-placed rocketed propelled grenade could kill and wound multiple defenseless marines. Camp Korean Village had few attack helicopters to speak of, only transport choppers. Air assistance was called; however, it was a good distance away. Nightfall was coming, and the insurgents would likely move yet the platoon would not have clearance to move themselves. With their vehicles shot to hell, they set up a watch and dug in so that at least some marines could try to sleep. Meanwhile, Third Platoon, expecting to be relieved, would be spending another cold night in the desert with little possibility of any rest and hot chow at least another day away.

CHAPTER 15

Balad Air Base was an Air Force–built and Air Force–managed military facility; and therefore, it was cleaner, newer, and had more amenities than most other US bases in Iraq. When Smitty arrived, it was midday, and the place was buzzing. He was amazed at how nice everyone and everything smelled. The staff looked healthier, from their clean teeth to tan skin all over (not just their faces). The chow halls were immaculate, and the base had several huge gyms for weightlifting, complete with treadmills and bikes. When he finally made it to the ward he would reside in, it was definitely a different vibe. The staff on duty looked tired and tried to stay positive; however, you could tell they had run out of positive, clever things to say to patients as more and more young men, and sometimes women, rolled in with serious injuries. The room Teddy was in had eight beds, and therefore, he would have seven roommates. Among the eight, he would be one of three marines along with four Army soldiers and one injured Navy corpsman. He took a quick look around the room as he was rolled in, trying to make an educated guess as to what the others' injuries were. He did not want to stare, and he knew that he would have plenty of time to get to know the other vets (assuming they wanted to talk about their experiences).

Smitty was able to glimpse enough of the other beds to see enormous amounts of gauze, legs in traction, IVs full of dripping meds, as well as men either sleeping in the middle of the day or looking exhausted because they had not been able to sleep. For the first time, baseball was completely out of the young warrior's mind. He knew he was not only lucky to be alive but very fortunate that his injuries were not worse. He had not lost any portion of any limb, at least not yet.

Camp Korean Village (Gateway to Jordan) was continuing to get colder by the day. The wind never seemed to stop and seemed to get angrier whenever a helicopter would take off from the little FOB for a mission. The positive for the marines of First Platoon was that the helo missions made the days go by a little quicker as opposed to just sitting on an OP (observation post) off the side of a road for four days. There were also no officers around to hassle the young marines as few officers wanted anything to do with the cold and the wind. As the weather grew worse and the holidays drew nearer, even the toughest marines and sailors couldn't help but become just a little bit more homesick. Most marines and sailors, when they returned to the rear, rushed to a computer every chance they got. Stevie was different. He really did not want to know what was going on back home as he really did not want to know what he was missing. He did, however, want to know the status of his lifetime friend and fellow marine, Teddy. Stevie reached out to his platoon commander, who knew nothing more than Stevie, and was directed to talk to the company commander. Major Horton, the Echo Company commander was congenial with Corporal McClanahan; however, he made it clear he had not heard anything and did not want to be bothered. As the frustrated, homesick, and cold marine exited the tent, Horton could sense one of his best marines was slipping and his focus was not entirely in the game.

"Hold on, Mac." As Stevie turned around to face the major, he was given a nod and some words that he needed to hear. "As soon as I hear something about Corporal Smith, I will find you personally, but I need you to stay focused and watch out for our youngest devil pups!"

Being a child of the Internet generation, Stevie wanted information instantly, and he knew that someone out there had an update on his wounded brother. So as many of the young platoon mates used the downtime to hit the gym or check Facebook or Myspace, Corporal Mac took the opportunity to send some e-mails to his parents back in Southeast Texas. Surely Teddy's parents were aware of the latest status of their son, and most likely, the McClanahans were checking in with the Smiths as often as reasonably possible. The time difference that seven thousand miles encompassed meant that he would not get an instant response, yet he knew his dad would tell him what he knew as discreetly as possible at a reasonable hour. As soon as Stevie hit Send, he immediately stumbled to his rack. He needed a shower, he needed a shave, yet that camouflage poncho liner inside his black cold-weather sleeping bag looked so enticing. He jumped in and was asleep before his head hit the pillow.

Stevie awoke for an early-morning mandatory formation where minimal word was passed prior to the platoon being cut loose until 1300. Many marines headed right back to their rack, some headed to the makeshift weight room at Camp KV, and the remainder of the platoon headed straight for the Internet café. As Mac waited in line for the restricted time he was allotted on a computer, he couldn't help but wonder how the guys in Vietnam and Korea kept sane without access to the Internet. Even as recently as Desert Storm, as he had learned, the deployed servicemen had no access to e-mail, to CNN.com, to any up-to-date news from the world or from their families. Even in 1991, the warriors had to rely on good old-fashioned snail mail, which took weeks to arrive and sometimes never made it at all. A brief smile came across his face as he realized his current existence was not that great, yet he was grateful for what he did, in fact, have, which was a nearly instantaneous twenty-four-hour connection with the real world and the motherland of Texas that he missed so badly. Hence as soon as Stevie was able to get on a computer, he shot a point-blank e-mail back to Harbor Lake, Texas, the warm, modest home of J. P. and Betty McClanahan. As soon as Stevie hit the Send button, he pushed his heavy tired body out of the chair, advised the marine on Internet watch that he was done, headed back to his rack, and as usual, was asleep before his head hit the pillow.

CHAPTER 16

J. P. McClanahan was not a big fan of the technology generation. He actually missed home lines and answering machines and doing things face-to-face. He also knew, though, he was very fortunate to have an Internet lifeline to his son so he could share news from home more often and do whatever he could to keep his son's spirits up.

JP was aware his son would not e-mail for about a four-day period and knew it had been about four days since he had heard from him. Therefore, he clicked on the computer and went to his e-mail inbox. Simply seeing his son's name on the title of an unread mail made JP's eyes light up. *He is still with us, he is still OK, and he is one more day closer to home.* He read through Stevie's e-mail and knew immediately he had to call Bill Smith. JP figured that the Smiths would update the McClanahans when they were ready and they had the time, yet JP owed it to his son to try to get up-to-date information on his son's best friend and fellow marine.

Bill Smith had become very dependent on his caller ID. Their phone rang constantly, and while he appreciated all the people sending their best wishes, they also wanted some privacy as they learned more about what their son had been through, where he was, and when they could see him. When the phone rang this particular time, Bill noticed the long name McClanahan. He appreciated that JP had not bothered him during this hectic time and also knew that JP and his son, Stevie, were deserving of an update given all the boys had been through together. Bill picked up the phone, and the two men traded some small talk about baseball, grilling out, and even the unusually chilly fall in Harbor Lake.

JP quickly got to the point though. "Bill, I understand if this is none of my business, but Stevie is asking about Teddy. For whatever reason, he is not getting any information over there at all, and he respectfully asked if you could tell him anything about Teddy. How bad is he hurt, where is he now, and when does he get to come home to Texas?"

Bill brought JP up-to-date and then advised him of what he had just been made aware of earlier in the day. "They are getting him out of that godforsaken country, JP. He has been deemed stable enough to send on to Germany. I can't give you an exact date. However, he should be at Ramstein Air Base in the next few days. It looks like we will be able to go see him there, JP. He's damn lucky. We are so lucky. I am so damn grateful that I will get to see my boy again."

They were both silent for a minute as JP was faced with the awful thought that something could still happen to Stevie, something worse, and he might not get the chance to see him ever again. With a lump in his throat, JP wrapped up the brief, mostly encouraging conversation. "Thanks for your time, Bill. I'm so happy to hear you will be seeing Teddy soon."

In the days following, the Smiths received word that Teddy would be remaining in Germany through the American Thanksgiving holiday. They were also told that arrangements could be made for them to travel to Ramstein and spend the holiday in person with their son. The proud parents' excitement was tempered only due to a conversation Bill knew he must have with Teddy at some point.

"What are you going to tell him about baseball?" Teddy's mother asked his father.

Teddy knew the conversation would come up quickly, and he knew he could try telling his son he was just lucky to be alive and that he should be thankful for that. He also knew that while Teddy had matured and likely realized how truly lucky he was at this point, Teddy had only ever talked about playing baseball for a living. This bummed Bill out momentarily, but he soon started daydreaming about going to watch games *with* his son instead of games his boy was playing in. He could now relax and just enjoy the beauty of the game without being so nervous about his son succeeding and enjoying himself.

John Kaminski knew about the joy of watching a game without vicariously feeling pressure while desperately hoping a loved one will succeed on the diamond. Kaminski had fallen into what he considered a privileged life by being paid to watch baseball. As a scout for nine seasons with several big-league organizations, he did not have to worry or care which team won most of the game he was watching. All he had to do was hope that he could find a player once in a while whom no one knew about, at least right away, or find a young ballplayer who really fit his clubs' needs at that particular time. He loved being able to call a high school or college player and tell him that he was being taken in the major league draft. His only disappointment was he did not ever get a chance to work with these players once he convinced the big-league club to take a chance on them. No, he had to begin working immediately looking for players for the following year's draft.

Kaminski had grown up in Houston and developed a love for college baseball, attending many games at both the University of Houston and Rice University; both teams had become outstanding programs and sent many players to pro ball. When Kaminski graduated from Spring Woods High School in 1985 at Spring Woods High, he had a decision to make. His original plan was to go play college baseball for several different schools, including Texas Tech, Texas A&M and the University of Texas, as his high school teammate and future Hall-of-Famer Roger Clemens had done. As his senior year of high school progressed, Kaminski began to hear from a growing number of professional scouts. He eventually made the agonizing decision to forgo college and sign a pro contract with the Atlanta Braves. Seven minor league years and two knee surgeries later, he was released by the Braves Organization for good and found no one with even a minimal interest in signing him for even next to nothing. It was a decision he had always regretted as he felt he would have had a blast being a college player.

Fast forward to 2004: Kaminski now had a Sunday night routine of listening to a major league game on radio while he read through line scores and previous scouting reports all the while and gave thought as to where his next road trip would take him and whom he would watch play. Would this be the trip he finds the next superstar? As Kaminski began to doze off in his absurdly tiny apartment near Fenway Park, his cell phone rang and displayed a 713 area code. *Who is calling me this late at night from Houston?* he wondered. *This can't be good news.*

Wayne Graham was a tough, gritty, physically fit seventy-year-old man who had never made a living outside baseball, drawing paychecks from the game one way or another since he was eighteen years old. Graham had made it all the way to the majors with the New York Yankees. In the early eighties, he had taken a job in the fledgling junior college ranks. He eventually turned San Jacinto Junior College in Houston into a national powerhouse while developing players such as Andy Petitte and Roger Clemens along the way.

Graham's tough-love, no-nonsense, yet successful style was quickly noticed by nearby Rice University. Rice University was a respected, elite national academic institution with little or no athletic success since before the big booster multimillion dollar coach model that now exists in college football. Rice had been very competitive on a regular basis in the '40s, '50s, and '60s but had fallen on hard times, trying to keep up in any sport with the absurd athletic budgets that existed at places like the University of Texas or Texas A&M University just down the road. The Rice alumni and administration remained very proud of their academic reputation but were longing for some athletic success again in any form possible.

Wayne Graham was subsequently hired in 1991, and by 1997, the school made its first appearance ever in the College World Series in Omaha, Nebraska. Graham took the Owls back to the CWS in 1999 and 2002, and then in 2003, little Rice University won the Division I national championship.

When Kaminski picked up the phone, Coach Graham was matter of fact, as always. "Kaminski, I need you down here in a couple of days. So do you want the job or not?"

A little taken aback, not only by Graham's style and his immediate job offer, Kaminski was immediately impressed with himself that Coach Graham even knew who he was! After an awkward silence, while he collected himself and tried to sound dignified, he replied, "Hell yes, Coach, I want the job. I'm on my way!"

CHAPTER 17

As the Smith family of Harbor Lake, Texas, were packing their bags for a long yet blessed trip to the heart of Europe to see their beloved son in Germany, the beloved son of the McClanahan family of Harbor Lake was looking forward to his Thanksgiving dinner of T-rats at the Camp Korean Village chow hall. Perhaps Stevie was just getting a little less picky or perhaps he had just grown accustomed to the food, but he seemed to think the chow was getting better at Camp KV. Besides, he was grateful for anything hot as it was already cold during the day out in Western Al Anbar and bitter at night, with the desert winds howling.

Smitty was growing accustomed to his sterile environment inside the sprawling base hospital at Ramstein Air Base. He couldn't help but marvel at how clean the place was and how new everything looked. Sitting in a TV lounge on the Sunday before Thanksgiving, Smitty spoke aloud to no one in particular: "Man, the Air Force must get all the DOD money. Everything is so damn new. Everything is so damn clean."

From across the room a salty Air Force combat controller who, although wounded, still had incredible hearing was able to make out Smitty's words perfectly but did not take offense. He looked in Smitty's direction and stated, "Well, devil dog, you know the Air Force philosophy, construct the nice buildings first and *then* ask Congress for more money, because you've got to have runways, right?"

Bill and Betty Lou Smith figured they would have to fly through a dozen places and stay somewhere overnight before they would eventually reach Germany. Much to their delight, the military had spared no expense and planned on getting them over the pond to Europe quickly and comfortably. The Smiths remained on the same plane all the way to Germany, although they did stop in New York for fuel and to add a few more passengers. The couple had to keep reminding themselves this was not a vacation and they may be facing a very distraught son whose dream of playing major league baseball was all but gone. Yet as they struck up conversations with several other parents who were also on the long flight, they heard of marines, soldiers, airmen, and soldiers who had been burned or who had lost a limb or sight or hearing. They knew their son was resilient and proud, but the sad stories of the other parents did not ease the anxiety of discussing the reality of the cold, hard truth that must be looked straight in the face.

Meanwhile on the ward, Teddy had been alerted his parents were coming to see him but was not given any specific itinerary or even an arrival date. Teddy had been staying positive outwardly and on the inside, but not knowing what was going on with his platoon was bothersome. Being away for a few days was a nice break, so to speak, but he was now getting that nagging feeling he was letting them down by not joining them on their now freezing patrols. His platoon mates obviously didn't share that sentiment at all, as their only frustration was not receiving any updates on Teddy's condition or his state of mind. Smitty had slipped off into a midafternoon daydream and was startled by a loud but pleasant voice.

"Corporal Smith, Corporal Smith," the young female army nurse repeated, "I know you're comfortable, but we need you to come out to the nurse's station, as we have a delivery we need you to sign for."

Number 5 was a little puzzled as he had never had to sign for any of the packages he had received in the past. He wondered, *what could this be, and who the heck is it from?* As he exited the room and turned the corner into the hallway, he immediately was fixed upon the unmistakable pearly whites of his favorite lady in the world—dear old Mom, in the flesh, all the way from Harbor Lake, Texas!

After a brief signature smile that accentuated her big cheeks, her beloved son immediately noticed her eyebrows and chin sink in a way that could only indicate a mother's intense sadness over seeing a child in pain—not just any child, but *her* child. Her dearest Teddy immediately sensed this and jumped out of his chair to reassure the only woman who had ever loved him unconditionally, "Mom, it's OK. It's OK, really. I'm fine, and I'm getting better every day." Connie couldn't delay her long-anticipated hug with her baby boy although, as she embraced him, Teddy could feel her head turning as she look into her husband Bill's eye for reassurance.

Bill gave his longtime bride a nod to try to ease her current angst but knew he needed to say something and was struggling for the words. "Our son is alive, Connie. We're very lucky. Teddy is coming home, honey. Our son is coming back to Texas. He made it!" With that, Bill felt as if he had spoken those words with a megaphone and it seemed as if the whole ward was staring at him. Had he said something wrong, something offensive? The bottom line was that no one knew what to say in these situations and there was no handbook, no way to ever prepare for days like this. They all knew they needed to end the initial meeting and get on with the visit— change the subject so to speak. Teddy turned to hug his dad and told his mom and pop, "Hey, let me show you around and give you the grand tour of the resort."

The trio enjoyed a dinner of steak and potatoes with salad plus dessert that was comparable to many classy downtown Houston restaurants. The Air Force was never a branch to cut corners when it came to expenses for chow halls, barracks and base housing, or recreational facilities. Stevie passed on to his parents the joke (not too far from the truth) that the USAF built the amenities first and *then* asked for more money for planes and runways. The spirits seemed high for Mom, Dad, and son, and if someone was faking it, then it wasn't very obvious.

Eventually though they knew they would have to discuss the uncomfortable subjects of the extent of Teddy's injuries and his future (or nonfuture) regarding the game of baseball. Teddy had played over this eventual conversation in his mind many times just as his dad had. Both Smith men wanted to get this conversation over with and wanted to show the utmost respect for each other in the process. Teddy decided to take the lead and to handle these subjects with authority just as he had handled a fastball during his starring days at the Harbor Lake High. "Mom, Dad, I am hurt, and I know I am hurt. I am going to be hurting for a while, and recovery won't happen overnight. I know baseball is pretty much over for me, and I will miss it badly. But I am alive, and I am going to have a good life. I'm going to get back to Texas and stay there for all my days. You know a ton of guys my age are hurt a lot worse than I am. A lot of guys my age are dead!"

After that, the subject was not broached for the rest of the visit. The family met with the medical staff, who were forthright about the prognosis of Teddy's recovery and explained walking won't be a problem, but putting pressure on the foot or running will likely be excruciating and not advised for the rest of the young marine's life. As his son's condition was discussed in detail, Bill Smith couldn't help but continue to glance over at his son and look for the heartbreak in his eyes.

He would not see what he expected as Teddy felt the glances and continued to nod to his dad and smile as if to say, "It's OK. It's OK. I'm going to be fine!" The staff went on to tell the family that the short-term goal was to transfer Teddy back to the States, hopefully by Christmas. Being a marine, Teddy would most likely be sent to the Naval Medical

Center San Diego first, and after arrival, a subsequent transfer could likely be arranged to the Brook Army Medical Center at Fort Sam Houston, just down the highway from Harbor Lake in San Antonio, Texas.

After a three day visit in Germany the elder Smith's began their voyage back to the States hoping that their son would soon follow. Teddy felt good about seeing his folks and explaining to his dad that he was coping well and that physically he may never be the same, but his heart was strong and he felt fortunate. Smitty was saddened, however, that his mother had barely said a word during the visit. She looked crushed every time she made eye contact with her son and seemed to feel very helpless. Bill asked his son one final question before they departed, wondering how his son's best friend was holding up in Iraq. "How is Stevie doing? Is there anything we can do for him?"

Smitty chuckled and recalled the two MRE postcards he had received from his buddy. "He wrote me and didn't say he was afraid or homesick or tired, only that he was freaking cold, cold, cold, cold. He said he had no idea the desert got this freaking cold and longed for the heat of South Texas!"

With this, he finally saw another smile on his mom's face, and they exchanged a happy hug as they were escorted to the flight line in order to travel back to the motherland, the great state of Texas.

CHAPTER 18

Much of Al Anbar Province had proved to be dangerous as advertised in late 2004. The cold weather did not seem to deter insurgents much as they continued to deem their self-worth in relation to how many innocent people and American troops they could kill. Far west, Al Anbar, west of Ar Rutbah, was eerily calm in December of 2004, with only minor skirmishes erupting. First Platoon spent many days running roadblocks and checking vehicles traveling down Highway 1, or Mobile as the Americans more commonly deemed it. It was clear to all the powers that be that foreign fighters were coming in virtually every day from Jordan and especially through Syria in northwestern Al Anbar. Unfortunately, there simply was no manpower or time to cover every entryway heading east into Iraq, and the duty seemed futile and most unglamorous to Stevie and his platoon mates. Is this really why they traveled across the world? they thought. To serve as border patrol or customs agents? They were marines who had trained for months to fight and were confident and ready, and they felt they were not contributing much to the effort and wondered why they couldn't be used elsewhere in this war-torn country?

First Platoon was subsequently advised that they needed to stay where they were in order to help provide security for the first-ever democratic Iraqi elections, which were slated for 30 January 2005, which happened to be Stevie's twenty-first birthday. What better way to celebrate, he thought, than to be in a war-torn, alcohol-free, frozen desert seven thousand miles from home. But he quickly erased any negative thoughts when he thought about his best buddy who had wounded limbs and may never be the same. Stevie knew he was lucky to be alive and was just three to four months from being back in the USA. Thanksgiving Day was the halfway point of the deployment, and the platoon was surprised with a meal of steak and shrimp put together by an air wing unit that was rotating out. It was a nice reprieve and well appreciated prior to a 0300 reveille and four more days outside the wire on frozen observation points, hoping that something would happen and they would see some meaningful action yet at the same time hoping nothing would happen at all.

With Christmas Day two weeks away, corporal Theodore Smith was made aware he would be departing Germany that evening and would eventually land in Washington, DC. After a brief stay, he would then be transferred to the Naval Medical Center San Diego, where he would join other marines and sailors from Afghanistan and Iraq trying to recover while remaining on active duty in a wounded warrior battalion. He was advised his stay in Washington, DC, would be short and routine and it would be best if his family met him in San Diego. Neither Teddy nor his parents were happy that an immediate stateside reunion was being discouraged yet heeded the request/advice and made plans to meet up for Christmas in Southern California. Smitty was going to push for the opportunity to rehab at Brooke Army Medical Center (BAMC) in San Antonio but knew he had to be patient and professional with his wishes. His parents, not understanding the huge number of casualties and all the logistics and costs, were mystified as to why he was not sent to BAMC in the first place. They were not about to complain regardless, as their son was coming home to the States and he was coming home alive.

On 23 December 2004, the Smith family of Harbor Lake, Texas, arrived at the Fisher House at Naval Medical Center San Diego, near the world-famous Balboa Park Zoo. The Fisher House was a facility built and maintained specifically for family members of wounded and ill servicemen and servicewomen being treated at nearby national medical centers. The Smiths were assigned a sponsor, Chief Petty Officer David Garcia, who made sure they were settled in and escorted them to the medical center where their son would be checking into that evening after arriving by plane across town on North Island Naval Station. Once he arrived and was examined and determined to be stable, he would be assigned a barracks room adjacent to the hospital. Teddy knew a slew of appointments and possible surgeries might follow, but in the meantime, he had more pertinent business to attend to. He needed to give his parents and sisters, Rhonda and Debbie, their first stateside welcome home hug. When they all met that night, he did so despite being drugged up and groggy, and goose bumps and tears filled the room. No one was thinking about what might have been anymore. Their only thoughts were of things they were going to do together when Teddy got back to Texas. His sisters expressed a sincere promise to their baby brother that the *first* thing they were doing was take him to a Texas country music concert in historic Gruene Hall on the Guadalupe River in New Braunfels, Texas. If you were a true Texan and you hadn't been to Gruene Hall, then you were cheating yourself. Texas had a music scene all its own, with musicians playing smaller venues and making a good living without relentlessly pursuing the big record contract or the Nashville lifestyle. These were guys (and gals) who got their start in college towns like Austin and College Station and Lubbock playing in front of their friends, and as they became more popular, they just kept playing those same towns with pleasure, only in bigger rooms with a few hundred or thousand more "friends."

Teddy grinned from ear to ear, thinking of a cold draft beer in Gruene Hall with pretty girls everywhere and Texas legends Robert Earl Keen or Roger Craeger or Pat Green on the stage. His thoughts drifted to all the times he had listened to Texas music over cold beers with his lifelong friend Stevie, and his smile slowly disappeared. "I can't go there without Stevie." He paused and looked up toward his sisters' faces. "We can't go until Stevie gets home. It wouldn't be right to be in Gruene without him!"

Across the world, at the same time, Stevie and his squad sat off the highway in between two mini mountain elevations they had dubbed Luckenbach after a timeless country song by legends Willie Nelson and Waylon Jennings. The boys broke out their little gas stoves and discreetly warmed up some ramen noodles, which had become their lifeline. Packs and packs were sent from home in care packages, and they really hit the spot when you were cold and hungry and longed for something with some taste. The combat action the platoon seemed to be craving seemed to be imminent as the scheduled elections neared. Camp Korean Village and the surrounding patrols had been subject to rapidly increasing mortar fire and many units in the area were discovering improvised explosive devices (IEDs). Fortunately, most were discovered before they were detonated. Stevie himself seemed to be a little more jumpy as he had fired at several vehicles that seemed to be getting pretty close to their convoys, fearful of the growing danger of vehicle-borne improvised explosive devices (VBIEDs)—a tactic used by insurgents where an insurgent determined to drive would slam his explosive-laden vehicle into other vehicles or buildings or crowds and taking down troops and, often, innocent locals with them on the path to premature senseless death.

On the evening of 24 December 2004 (Christmas Eve back in the States), Stevie was part of a four-man fire team that pushed out from Luckenbach in a Humvee and discreetly hid in a ditch on the outskirts of Ar Rutbah, looking for any suspicious characters coming in or out of town after dark. Once the men were settled in a tactical location, the leader of the patrol, a crusty sergeant from New England named Williams, determined they would have one man standing and alert panning the area while the other three rested. They would rotate in ninety-minute intervals, and the resting marines would be awoken if there was any traffic, by foot or vehicle, in the area. Stevie thought that perhaps they should have two men up while two slept, but he was cold and tired and was happy he would not have the first watch. He would be the third man up and would be able to sleep for three hours before having to crawl out of his sleeping bag and poncho liner and back into the chill of another cold desert winter night. Stevie was to be awoken by a motivated yet tiny in stature lance corporal named Tran, the youngest son of a father who had risen to the rank of master chief in the South Vietnamese Navy and escaped to the USA just before the fall of Saigon to North Vietnam. One of the things Stevie loved about the military was the people he met and served with from all over the country. He never would have a chance to learn of so many people's backgrounds in any other line of work.

At approximately 0030 hours on 25 December 2004 (thirty minutes into Christmas Day in Mesopotamia), Stevie happened to roll over on his rubber sleeping mat while sleeping on the ground next to the front tire of the Hummer. As the bright moon of this night forced his eyes open ever so slightly, he caught what appeared to be a man hunched over the hood. Stevie rose up slowly while simultaneously pulling his M16 rifle out of his warm sleeping bag. As he continued to rise ever so slightly, the figure became more and more clear. He know knew the body was Lieutenant Corporal Tran, yet the young Asian American was so still and quiet it was not obvious if the marine was sleeping or dead. Stevie leaned toward Tran with his ear while his eyes continued to scan the perimeter. The night was eerily quiet without even the normal barking of stray dogs, and therefore, Stevie was able to pick up the relaxed breathing of the lance corporal and determine he was in fact alive. Now Stevie had to decide whether to wake him and risk noisily startling him or let him sleep. Stevie chose to assume the watch while angrily stewing over Tran's dereliction of duty. They could have all had their throats slashed because of Tran, and the higher-ups should know about Tran's failure to properly hand over the watch duty. About one hour into his now two-hour watch, he decided he would privately ream out Tran but not report what he had done (or not done). Stevie knew one thing for sure, he would find a way out of any further squad-team sized (four- to five-man) night patrols if at all possible or would sure as hell insist on two marines being awake at all times! *What a lousy way to spend Christmas,* he thought as he began to feel depressed. He quickly caught his snap, and his morale shot up, knowing that he had made it through Thanksgiving and Christmas and Echo 2/7 was now in the homestretch of their deployment.

The first several weeks of January were windy and dusty and especially cold and seemed to limit friendly coalition patrols and insurgent activity alike. About this time, the company received word that another unit would be flying west to support Echo 2/7. There would be at least one platoon of marines from First Battalion, Third Marine Regiment, flying out from Al Asad to assist with security and patrols during the anticipated period of tension. The battalion was based in Hawaii and had to be itching to return to Oahu sooner rather than later. Like 2/7, the Hawaiian marines were slated to return home soon. In fact, they were actually scheduled to return home in late February, but tragically, that would not be early enough.

CHAPTER 19

Twenty-eight January 2005 was a largely quiet day across Iraq, including the almost always volatile Al Anbar Province. Coalition troops across the country knew that violence was inevitable with the coming election scheduled for 30 January. Yet an eerie calm again existed as it seemed that there was an unwritten understanding between the insurgents and the troops that everyone could rest up and stay warm on the days leading up to 01/30/05.

Second and Third Platoon of Bravo Company, First Battalion, Third Marine Regiment, were slated to fly from Al Asad Air Base to Camp Korean Village on 28 January in order to support election security. Second Platoon flew out as planned midday on 28 January, and it was decided that the third platoon helo flight would be staggered until the evening for security reasons as well as heightened wind speeds that afternoon. A night flight meant cooler temps for Third Platoon, as sunlight would not help reduce the chilly temps, although it also meant one more meal at the pristine Al Asad chow halls. CH53 helicopter flights meant a large opening on the side of the aircraft for a gunner, which allowed blistering cold air and wind to fly through the helo at will. The rear of the helicopter housed the ramp where the passengers boarded and disembarked. This was also left down for both a sight line for the gunner and for the troops to exit hastily if necessary. On many a flight, several marines could be seen trying to assume the fetal position to block the cold or even locking arms with another marine as they rotated, blocking the wind for each other in an attempt to make the flights less miserable.

Captain Lenny McIlhenny, a native of Alvin, Texas, and a graduate of Texas A&M as well as his copilot Miles Franklin, a TCU graduate from Arlington, Texas, watched the twenty-seven US marines and one navy corpsman board the aircraft just shy of 2000 hours (8:00 p.m.) local time. With the flight crew of four marines, the flight manifest marked a total of thirty-two packs, three marine officers, twenty-eight enlisted marines, and one enlisted sailor. The navy corpsman aboard, Johnny Tower, had a name befitting his build. Petty Officer Tower had had been a highly recruited offensive tackle from Hinsdale, Illinois. The towering presence, who stood six feet five, felt the calling to serve after two years on scholarship at Ohio State. He actually had to slim down by forty pounds in order to gain acceptance into the US Navy. Johnny Tower had originally planned to return to school after serving his four years and become a football coach. After three years as an enlisted man, he had decided he had an ability to lead and help young sailors and marines. He had begun the process of applying for Navy and Marine Corps commissioning programs, and a promising career as an officer looked like a genuine possibility. The men aboard the CH53 ranged in age from nineteen to forty-three; they were all tired and cold and ready to go home. At 2017 hours, McIlhenny and Franklin lifted the bird vertically and began the westward flight to Camp Korean Village. They would never arrive at their planned destination.

No one will ever know what truly happened. The pilots maintained radio contact for nearly forty minutes and were approximately thirty to thirty-five minutes from east of the town of Ar Rutbah when they were last heard from. The night was not rainy, but lightning flashes filled the air. There were no reports of enemy muzzle flashes, mortars, or RPG fire anywhere in the area. Yet something or someone made that bird go down, and thirty-two brave American souls were never making it back to American soil.

Stevie happened to be taking his turn on radio watch from 0200–0400 when he heard traffic on the radio.

"We have an unaccounted for friendly aircraft in the area; requesting units to proceed to grid."

A grid number location followed. Stevie began to focus and comprehend what his tired ears seemed to be hearing.

The next radio transmission was chilling: "TRAP platoon QRF dispatch. I say again, TRAP platoon QRF, proceed to last known location of aircraft."

TRAP stood for "tactical recovery of aircraft personnel—quick reaction force." Stevie immediately awoke fully and realized that a US helicopter had gone down and it had likely gone down within five kilometers of his platoon's position. He knew what he had to do and began the process of awaking the squad members around his truck. He made contact with the platoon sergeant, and as an awkward silence filled the group, the marines saddled up for what may be a grisly mission. Normally, marines may bitch out loud about being awoken in the middle of the cold night, but this was no time to complain. They had brothers in need, brothers who were in trouble and who might not be able to be bailed out this time!

The four-vehicle convoy headed east just off Highway 1–Mobile, staying about five hundred meters off the pavement and on the dirt to avoid any possible IEDs. As the bright moon began to illuminate the night, the turret gunners began to see neat patterns of smoke twirling up in the sky about one kilometer ahead. The convoy inched closer, and turret gunner Jolando Price, a lean, laid-back Californian, saw what he thought was a part of a propeller.

Before he could say anything, the driver of the lead vehicle, Daniel Othon, a Mexican American from the Arizona desert, looked out his window and confirmed, "It's one of the props, man, nowhere near the rest of the bird. I think they're all toast, man. I think they're all gone!"

The next few minutes seemed to occur in slow motion. The five-ton truck Stevie was riding in crept further forward, and the tragic event was instantly humanized. Stevie looked down and saw the reflection of a wrist watch. As his eyes followed the arm up, it led to a partially charred body lying face down. Stevie began to think about how awful the last moments must have been for these brave souls. His eyes scanned the immediate area, and no other bodies were immediately visible. Maybe they all survived? Maybe this was the only casualty? As the vehicle slowed to halt, the grim reality was exposed; the marines could now see reflections of aircraft parts, Kevlar helmets, and exposed skin illuminated by headlights and the moon. Ominously, the men began to dismount the vehicle when the call came over the radio that they had received a reprieve from the dreadful task of cleaning up a crash site and placing thirty-two brothers in body bags. Second Platoon was ordered to return to their positions (observation posts) along the highway. Third Platoon would be sent out immediately from behind the wire at Camp Korean Village. Second Platoon would be spared this awful duty, yet it didn't seem to lessen the blow one bit. The men were shaken, and they felt extremely mortal. They knew the fallen were weeks from going home and had not made it out. At the moment, First Platoon, to a man, did not like their chances of all making it home either.

On 30 January 2005, the same day his lifelong friend Stevie McClanahan was turning twenty-one years old thousands of miles from home in the Middle East, Corporal Theodore Smith was airborne en route back to the motherland, the great state of Texas. Smitty wasn't going all the way to his beloved Harbor Lake but was going to be pretty darn close. His new home for a while would be at the newly remodeled Brook Army Medical Center

(BAMC) at Fort Sam Houston in San Antonio, Texas. The medical center now included a multi-multimillion dollar rehabilitation facility known as the Center for the Intrepid. Smitty had heard about the facility somewhat from his cousin, Gary Otto, who had been involved in the mammoth construction project.

A day after being given a room at BAMC, Smitty was provided a tour of the Intrepid Center and was utterly amazed. Once again he felt goose bumps and an enormous appreciation for the unwavering support the American people continued to provide for today's US Armed Forces. His mind slipped back not only to the way Stevie's dad had been treated coming back from Vietnam but more so to the way the Vietnam War wounded had been forced to recover, in disgusting VA hospitals under the glare of an angry, unsympathetic public who blamed the innocent, broken veterans for the horrors of the eternal Vietnam conflict. Teddy knew he could not possibly look every Vietnam veteran in the eye and apologize for the way they had been treated, yet he knew for a fact that from now on, he would take the opportunity to look every 'Nam vet in the eye, shake their hand, and thank them for their incredibly difficult and selfless service.

The following day, with his dad and mom preparing to return to Harbor Lake at his insistence, Number 5 was introduced to his suitemate. As the men prepared to shake hands, they both did a double take simultaneously.

"Smitty, is that you?"

"Yeah, it's me, Sims. What the hell are you doing here?"

Robbie Sims was a flame throwing six-feet-five lefty from Kingwood Park High School outside Houston who had graduated from high school a year after Smitty and Stevie. Smitty and Sims had played on several traveling all-star teams together during their teenage summers. Sims had been drafted by the Chicago Cubs in 2003 in the third round, and Smitty had assumed Robbie had signed and was working his way through the minors.

Sims went on to explain he felt that the Cubs had lied to him about the potential terms of his contract, backsliding at the last minute. Sims stated his dad thought he should go play D1 college ball for three years and then take a crack at pro ball, as by that time, he would be more mature and closer to a shot at the majors. Sims told Smitty that he was about to decide between offers from Texas A&M, Rice, and oddly enough, Michigan State (he liked the Spartan uniforms they wore) when he heard about Teddy's decision to put off pro ball to serve in the USMC.

Smitty was speechless yet again and then looked up at Sims. "You mean to tell me you turned down all that money because of me?"

As Sims began to chuckle, he replied, "Don't give yourself too much credit, Smitty. I was thinking about it anyway. My dad was an army ranger before I was born, and my grandpa was an army ranger in Korea. They never said much about it, but I think me serving in the military makes them more proud than baseball ever did."

Sims had enlisted as a combat engineer and had ended up in the first battle of Fallujah at nineteen years old. With the first wave rolling into town, he had fallen victim to the first blast heard by anyone. Three soldiers from his vehicle were killed instantly, and Sims was thrown an estimated one hundred feet. Sims was extremely lucky that no major organs were penetrated by shrapnel and that none of his limbs were affected either, meaning no amputation.

"It's my head," Sims told Smitty. "My head never stops hurting, my memory sucks, and my damn vision is always blurry."

Smitty just nodded, not knowing what to say next or how to comfort his former opponent. After another long pause, Smitty asked the inevitable question: "What about baseball? Can you still play, man, or is it over for you?"

"You know, it's funny, Smitty. I can't remember what happened a week ago, but I remember every game I ever played!" After the two young men forced another half-smile and exchanged another half nod Sims continued, "But I tell you what: someone is going to take me, man. Even if it is some Podunk junior college in Idaho, someone will give a chance. So nah, I'm not done playing, brother, not yet!"

Smitty felt uplifted and wanted to talk to his old buddy Stevie Mac that instant. He couldn't pick up the phone and just call Stevie, considering the circumstances Stevie was in, but knew Stevie could retrieve e-mail pretty often. "Hey, slick," he stated as he turned to Sims, "we don't have to report to anyone until tomorrow right, so what do you say lets hit the Internet café and then go into the San Anton River Walk, have some beers, and talk baseball?"

"Sure thing," affirmed Sims. "But what do you need to do on the Internet that can't wait?"

"I want to e-mail my old buddy Stevie Mac and tell him who I ran into!"

"McClanahan?" Sims asked, and after receiving a smile and a nod from Smitty, Sims couldn't help but ask, "Can that smart son of a bitch hit a curveball yet?"

With a chuckle and a shake of the head a rejuvenated Teddy Smith responded as they left the passageway and headed out of the building, "Well, he is still smart, but, no, he still can't hit a curveball! Tell you what though: you don't have to hit a curveball to be a senator or a CEO whatever that son of a bitch is going to end up as!"

CHAPTER 20

One of the advantages of playing baseball in the South was having the option of outside practices and hosting actual games by middle February on your home field. The tradeoff to dealing with Houston summers was having the mild winters and being able to golf (and play baseball) just about year-round. As the Rice University Baseball team took the field for the first time on February 17, 2005, it was seventy degrees in Houston, and morale and expectations were, as usual, very high around the program. Rice was just two years removed from winning a national championship in Omaha, Nebraska, and was opening the season against their biggest rival, the 2004 national champion University of Texas Longhorns.

For the newest member of the Rice University family, the feeling of bliss was evident to all around him. For assistant coach John Kaminski, the smile was from ear to ear, as he had found his calling. Kaminski knew if he could remain a part of this program, learn from the best there is in Coach Wayne Graham, then he would likely never have to go back to corporate America. Graham had given Kaminski the title of recruiting coordinator. Coach Graham wanted Coach Kaminski to be present at every game, but between games, he was to be on the road recruiting high school and junior college baseball players who could help Rice baseball maintain its pattern of almost annual trips to the College World Series in Omaha. Kaminski had no complaints, as to him, the game of baseball was still the American pastime. Kaminski would watch baseball and talk baseball and write about baseball every day for free, and now he was getting paid for it!

Coach Graham had given his newest assistant an interesting challenge, however, as Graham felt his program was slipping back behind the University of Texas as the second best program in the state while also watching other programs in the state, such as TCU and Texas A&M, making College World Series appearances as one of the final eight teams standing at the end of the college baseball season in June. Graham advised Kaminski he needed to start going after unconventional recruits. By *unconventional*, he meant guys perhaps playing in Puerto Rico or perhaps guys who had been injured their senior year and given up on baseball a little early. Of course, there were always gems who had blossomed late and were hidden while playing for a remote junior college in Idaho or Rhode Island, but most four-year colleges had plans in place to find those guys. *What about the guys,* Graham pondered, *that were a little older?* Guys who had not started their college eligibility yet, maybe who sat out for family reasons, or maybe put off college for something noble such as the military? As Coach Graham was finishing up describing this task to John Kaminski, a lightbulb was going off in the new coach's head.

"Coach, I'll get started on this right away, but I won't be in tomorrow." Before Graham could protest, Kaminski continued, "It's important, Coach. I'll just be gone a day, and I'll explain later, but there is just something I need to check on."

After a distrusting nod from Coach Graham, Kaminski headed back to his apartment to do a little research. He had to find an address in preparation for a short road trip. Ignoring a couple voice-mails regarding invites to a local pub, Kaminski eventually found what he was looking for, sort of. He couldn't find a phone number of the folks he planned to visit and felt uneasy, as he believed in calling before showing up whenever possible. However, he found an address he believed to be good and set his alarm for the next day. After some coffee in the morning he would be headed out to the suburbs, to a place called Harbor Lake, Texas.

Mid-February in Iraq saw the first snowfall the marines from 2/7 had seen during their tour. Morale was high among the marines from Echo Company as they had been told that they would be going home as planned in late March, and there would be no extension of their deployment. The high morale and excitement was deflated immensely when the marines were called together on 18 February by the company commander aboard Camp Korean Village. The marines knew something had happened in their area of operation as the Internet had been down for several days, which normally meant next of kin had to be notified. Major Horton informed the Echo marines that eight marines from the battalion had been killed in the last forty-eight hours. Two separate vehicles from the battalion's Fox and Weapons Companies had been blown up by IEDs in Al Anbar Province. Each vehicle had four marines inside, and there were no survivors.

To a man, every marine and sailor who heard these words was dead silent. The battalion had over sixty wounded to date, but until yesterday had not suffered any killed in action (KIA). Now five weeks from the date they were scheduled to go home, these marines, just like the victims of the helo crash several weeks ago, would never be going home!

Major Horton advised the marines of what should have gone without saying at that moment, "You can't get drop your packs yet boys, you can*not* become complacent! We're still in a war zone, gentlemen. We're STILL in a war zone. You gents have been through enough here, and you have done a great job. Does anyone here really want to be a part of a memorial service before we leave?"

It was a rhetorical question, and Horton expected no answer. However, as he scanned his audience, he took notice that while no one spoke up, he saw over a hundred heads swinging left and right to indicate the universal sign of *no*. What the marines and sailors were really thinking was hell no, that didn't sound appealing to any single one of them! The major went on to tell them that they would be departing the country in the next five weeks, but he couldn't tell them an exact date for OPSEC.

"Don't you dare speculate on an exact date, say five weeks from today, and start e-mailing your family or your putting everyone's ass at risk," exclaimed Horton. "Not just all ours but your replacements'. When 3/7 [Third Battalion, Seventh Marine Regiment] starts rolling in, you better tell them everything you know and show them the ultimate respect, just as 1/7 did for you. You want to tell your families when you're coming home, then tell them by the end of March. Our people in the rear will get them a date a few days out, but if you e-mail any specific dates or talk about any date on the phone, you will be standing tall before the BC [battalion commander]!"

With that, the company CO dismissed the men, and of course, they were racing one another to the Internet café. After waiting about thirty minutes, Stevie McClanahan was able to get to a computer and open up his e-mail. Before he had a chance to send a new message, he noticed he had sixty new messages, and most of them weren't junk. *Had it been that long since I've been on the net?* He wondered silently. *Have things been that crazy?* He knew the answer as he the platoon had been very active with patrols and trying to secure their AO (area of operation) before their replacements came in and the RIP (reinforce in place) turnover began in earnest. Stevie felt good about the fact he had so many e-mails and that people back home had been worried about them, concerned since he had not been in touch and wanting to know nothing had happened to him. He quickly perused his inbox, knowing that in his thirty-minute allotted

Internet time, he would not be able to open or possibly respond to sixty e-mails.

One e-mail immediately jumped out to Stevie, as it was eloquently titled "HEY NUMNUTS!" This had to be from the one and only Teddy Smith of Harbor Lake, Texas. Stevie began to grin from ear to ear while double clicking the title to open the e-mail. He knew that Smitty must not be doing too poorly if he had his smart-ass sense of humor back. Smitty began his e-mail in typical fashion, extremely similar to the messages he had sent Stevie before he was injured. In his first e-mail to his old friend since he was injured, Smitty opened the text with "Buttmuncher, while you are over there wasting taxpayers' money with your poor shooting, I am back here in the motherland (old Tejas) trying to recover. Anyway, you benchwarmer, you will never guess who I ran into. My freaking roommate here is Robbie Sims, from Kingwood; guess he never signed with the Cubs and became an Army Ranger. I had no idea, did you? Anyway, he got blown up over there too. He looks as tough as ever, but he says his head is all jacked up; says his vision is all fuzzy from the blast. You know something though, man? He told me he wants to play ball again now more than ever. He told me he had forgotten how much he loved the game and did not have any idea how much he would miss it. Sims says when he is discharged he is going to write to some junior colleges and see if he can get his playing career going one more time, and I'm not betting against him! It got me to thinking though, man; what if we gave it one more go?? I mean I know I'm jacked up, but who knows, with therapy, maybe someone will give me one more chance; we could walk on together somewhere, man. I mean, we will have our GI Bill, right? And our parents won't have to pay for it? Why not, man? I mean, we have done our time in the corps, we served our country; did more than most people do for Uncle Sam. Am I crazy or selfish to be thinking like this brother? I respect your opinion like no one else's. Do you think baseball is over for me?"

Stevie leaned back in his chair and pondered the heavy question his longtime friend had just thrown at him. Smitty had always seemed indestructible to him. Even though he had known him for so long, his childhood pal had always seemed larger than life. Stevie had been focusing on the task at hand, which was staying alive and watching out for his junior marines and had not had the time or energy to think about the future as of late. Stevie had been certain he wanted to attend an Ivy League school and had accepted the fact baseball was over for him. But perhaps he had a higher calling? Stevie knew that baseball was everything to Teddy Smith and that if it was taken away from him then Number 5's postwar recovery would be even more difficult. Were Smitty's thoughts so crazy? Was there a college out there who would give a guy a shot who hadn't picked up a bat or glove in three years? Stevie had always considered himself fortunate to be academically gifted but had also always been jealous of people like Teddy, to whom athletics success seemed to come so easily. *Just get home,* he thought as he mumbled to himself. "Just get home and *then* you will have options!"

As Stevie finally snapped out of his daydream and began to hit the reply button, much to his shock, he heard the dreaded words of every visitor to the Internet café, "Computer 3, *your time is up."*

CHAPTER 21

Billy Smith was a hardworking blue-collar man who made more money than most people in Harbor Lake realized he did. He had volunteered to work the night shift some time ago in order to make an even better wage. Billy also enjoyed the serenity of quiet weekdays at home by sleeping in, watching the news, taking long walks around the quiet neighborhood, and reading the paper at the coffee shop or in the backyard, page by page, as slowly as he desired. The only bummer was actually falling asleep after ingesting a good amount of caffeine every night shift. He normally arrived home at about 6:30 a.m. and after reading most of his paper would fall into his rack at about 8:30 a.m. On this particular day, he was just slipping into la-la land at about 8:35 when he thought he heard the doorbell ring. As he rolled over to ignore it and fall into a deep sleep, he heard the bell again. *This couldn't be good news,* he thought. One hundred percent of his friends and relatives knew he worked evenings, and his remote cul-de-sac house had several large No Soliciting signs. Word had pretty much gotten around to the door-to-door salesmen that even if they kept knocking, he would just wave them off from his window and even banged on the window with his pistol when one persistent and desperate sales rep would not go away easily.

Due to years of working in the dark and avoiding too much sunlight or other damaging factors to his eyes, Bill still had the keen eyesight of a sniper. Therefore, as he peered through the window to the left of his door, despite being groggy, he could clearly see a sharp-dressed, well-proportioned gentleman who, oddly, was wearing a large blue cap with the word RICE spelled out in large blue letters across the front. *Is this some nerd from Rice University raising money for the library?* he thought.

Bill took a deep breath and tried to convince himself he would be initially polite and would get ugly with the unannounced visitor only if necessary, and then slowly cracked the door partially open. *"Yeah?"* Bill exclaimed giving the stranger no doubt to the fact that he needed to state his business immediately and be on his way shortly afterward.

"Mr. Smith?"

"Yeah, I'm Mr. Smith. Who the hell are you, and what do you want?"

"Mr. Smith, I'm John Kaminski. I'm with the Rice University Baseball Program, and I—"

Before Kaminski could get another word out, Bill interrupted and exclaimed, "You must be an *idiot.* My son doesn't even play baseball anymore. He is in the Marine Corps, and he has been wounded, so I'll ask you again, what the hell do you want?"

"Mr. Smith, I know your son is in the Marine Corps, and I was sorry to hear of his injuries, but, sir, I don't think his playing career is over. Sir, I believe he can still play the game!"

After a long awkward pause and a deep breath, Bill's suspicion began to melt slowly, and he cracked the door further, "Come in, Mister—?"

"Kaminski, John Kaminski. But please call me John, sir."

With a chuckle, Bill responded, "I appreciate the *sir* bit. That's mighty respectful of you. But you're an adult. Please feel free to call me Bill."

"Thank you, sir—ah, I mean, Bill. I'm a new assistant baseball coach with Rice, and I've been tasked with finding us some big-time players, guys that will help us keep our program at the level we expect.

"Mr. Bill, when Coach Graham told me to go find players, your son was the first guy I thought of! He was born to be a ballplayer. He was meant to be on a baseball diamond! Sir, I would like to respectfully request your permission to speak with him in person. Maybe we could get him on campus for a year or two and see how his rehab is going?"

Bill's head began to slowly nod, increasing speed ever so slightly, and a smile was slowly starting to form on his crusty, leathering face.

Kaminski took this as a signal that said "Go on." Therefore Kaminski proceeded, "The Texas Medical Center is right next door to our campus, sir. There are five of the finest hospitals in the world right there. Whatever the VA won't pay for, our athletic department will find a way to cover. We're a small school, Mr. Smith, but we have a ton of very successful alumni and the second biggest endowment in the country behind Harvard! We can take care of your son, Mr. Smith. You have my word!"

Bill did not know exactly what Kaminski meant by *endowment,* but he knew Rice graduates made an awful nice living. He knew if Teddy were able to earn a degree from Rice, someday, he would be sitting pretty. But more importantly, Bill knew his son loved baseball, and he knew Rice was a solid Division I nationally recognized elite program. Bill thought if Teddy could just be affiliated with the program in some form or fashion, he could break into coaching baseball, which would be the closest he may ever come to playing the game again. Bill had never talked to Teddy about coaching before because they had both assumed he would actually be playing the game professionally for many years to come.

"You said your first name was John, correct?"

"Yes, sir—ah, I mean, Bill—yes, my name is John."

"John, if you're really serious about this, I'm wondering if you can wait a few weeks until my son is released from the hospital and gets a chance to come home for a while. I don't want anyone going to see him while he is still hospitalized and messing with his head, you know what I mean?"

"Of course, of course, Mr. Smith. I only came here to ask your permission to speak with your son. I didn't think it would be appropriate to sneak up on him without talking to you first."

"OK, John, they're telling me he may be able to come home and stay at least for a while 'bout the end of March."

"Bill, would you mind giving me a call when he gets back and maybe let me know how soon I could come see him?"

"You have my word, John. After he has been home for a couple days, I'll get in touch with you; look forward to seeing you again."

"I appreciate that very much, sir—I mean, Bill—and I just want to say, not only do I appreciate your son's service to the country, but I sincerely appreciate yours as well."

Bill Smith initially seemed puzzled and wondered how Kaminski had even known about the fact he was a military vet. Bill's eyes glanced down to his own massive forearm and the tattooed caduceus, which was the medical symbol representing service in the enlisted Naval Hospital Corps.

Kaminski's eyes went the same direction and then rotated to the old pictures on the wall of Bill in uniform during his time in Vietnam.

The old navy vet became a little choked up and responded with a nod. "Thank you, John. I don't hear that very often. When I came home, I didn't hear that at all!"

With that, Coach Kaminski headed out the Smith's front door, feeling good about the visit and feeling lucky to be alive. Baseball was still the national pastime to John Kaminski, and he was thrilled as hell to be a part of it.

CHAPTER 22

"The last full month and it is not even a *full* month" was the conversation between First Platoon marines aboard Camp Korean Village. Echo Company, along with the remainder of the battalion had been told they would be stateside *before* the end of March. This wasn't a leap year, so February had only its twenty-eight days as a small obstacle before it was *return* to CONUS month. The marines and corpsmen of First Platoon were taking to heart the talks of avoiding complacency and had the news of the battalion's recent killed in action (KIA) numbers fresh in their head. Not only were the marines being extra vigilant outside the wire on patrols, however. They were taking steps to avoid getting in trouble during their last few weeks in garrison. Marines were dumping smuggled-in alcohol packages sent from friends and relatives in Scope or ketchup bottles. Marines were deleting or trashing anything remotely offensive on their computers or hard copies of any smut they may have accumulated.

Alas, one unfortunate marine from Echo Company would not be heading home with the same rank he arrived in-country with. The hope among most deployed marines is to get promoted, "pick up a stripe," during their "pump," or at least go home with the rank they came with. One sure way to lose a stripe or get demoted was to be guilty of a negligent discharge. After every patrol, the marines cleared their weapon into a barrel appropriately named "the clearing barrel." A marine needed to pull out the clip of twenty-nine M16 (5.56 millimeter) rounds and then eject the thirtieth round, which was already chambered and ready to be fired. This is a process described as going from *condition 1 to condition 4*. When outside the wire, the marines were always in *condition 1* or "locked and loaded". Once inside the wire, they would go back to condition 4 with no round or magazine in the weapon. Unfortunately for Lance Corporal Danny Nathan, he had forgotten about the round already chambered and thought he was actually in *condition 3* (magazine inserted in the weapon with all thirty rounds and *no* round actually chambered). Nathan was obviously worn down from standing a midnight-to-0200 watch on the side of a cold road; however, he knew better, and after releasing his magazine, he somehow had his weapon off safe and was just playing with the trigger as he was exiting his Hummer, and the bullet went right between the two marines in the front seat and, by the grace of the God, hit the windshield and not the marines themselves.

Nathan was obviously horrified of what could have happened and actually relieved when it was announced by the company commander he would only be losing one rank and would be going home a private first class (PFC).

Major Horton was obviously incensed that a young marine could lose his focus in such an irresponsible manner yet knew if the marine was "put on blast" to a major degree, he may completely shut down and may not make it home at all. The incident was a scare but another needed wakeup call and yet one more reminder for the marines and sailors of Echo Company that their tour was *not* over.

Corporal Stephen P. McClanahan was burned out and struggling to stay motivated and continued to daydream in awe about the men in Vietnam who did twelve- and thirteen-month tours seeing combat virtually every day. He remained beyond awestruck when he thought of the soldiers, sailors, airmen, and marines who left home early in World War II only to return home after three years—*years*, he kept thinking. Was he just part of the "wussifcation" of America, or were those men just that incredible? He had to remind himself that all men have their breaking points, but also, so many step up way beyond their known abilities and courage levels when faced with the prospect of letting others down. Perhaps he was overthinking this, yet thinking was exactly what he needed to do the for twenty-three days and a wake-up until Echo Company would leave for Kuwait and, two weeks later, the continental United States.

By this time, the platoon had a somewhat safer mission, although it was disgusting. The platoon would still leave the wire for four nights a week, sleeping out in the elements. The four-night ops no longer included foot patrols within the city limits of Ar Rutbah, except on rare occasions, and instead involved the platoon vehicles being set up in an overwatch position outside town, right in the middle of a huge trash dump. As one can probably imagine, there were no incinerators or recycling centers in this remote western Al Anbar city, therefore, the residents simply drove or walked about a mile outside of town and dumped in the previously open desert that was now a huge trash-infested area covered in filth, odor and inhabited by hundreds of stray dogs. The marines actually found the place tranquil, though, even with the dogs howling at night.

As February wound down, several snowfalls came and covered the dump and made them all forget where they were laying their heads. The cold also seemed to keep the majority of the flies and mosquitoes away despite all the refuge. The platoon was called in for quick reaction force (QRF) from time to time, at which point they had to jump in their vehicles and fly into town, responding to suspicious activity. Normally, the loud bang that set off the QRF was just an old Iraqi vehicle in need of maintenance that would backfire. The ground-pounders of First Platoon had been receiving a great deal of air support of late from a nearby base in Al Qaim, near the Syrian border. The helos (and, occasionally, jets) would fly over the region to include Ar Rutbah and look and listen for suspicious activity. The presence of Echo Company as well as their brothers from the Third Light Armored Reconnaissance Battalion (LAR) for the past seven months had really calmed the area around Ar Rutbah and significantly lowered the number of insurgent crossings over the formerly porous Jordanian Iraqi border.

The boys were feeling pretty good as their second-to-the-last four-day field op was coming to a close on 01 March 2005, as the general unspoken feeling was the platoon would be exposed to no further combat and not have to witness any more injuries or death, friend or foe. This is why the events of that evening were all the sadder and, likely, completely unnecessary!

At approximately 1800 hours, on 01 March, just as the desert sun was beginning to set on a fairly warm day and a crisp air started to form under a moonless sky, the platoon headed east into town instead of west toward Camp Korean Village. Expecting to be relieved and enjoy some warm tents, Internet, and good chow, the platoon was told to dismount their vehicles and begin a foot patrol right through the heart of Ar Rutbah, Al Anbar, Iraq. Not a word was said by any of the enlisted marines who all had the same thoughts: *What are we doing here, and why? How long is this damn patrol going to last, and when are we going back to the FOB and hitting the hot showers?* Before the marines knew it, they had formed a cordon around the town square and were setting up vehicle checkpoints from four different directions, stopping every vehicle that was coming into downtown or trying to head to the city's outskirts. Stevie would never find out who had given the order or why the patrol had been deemed necessary—there would be an investigation, but no one would end up asking Stevie's opinion of the matter.

At approximately 1815 hours, just as the checkpoints were beginning in earnest, a small old red Chevrolet S-10 pickup truck with a trailer installed over the bed came onto the horizon, heading north to south right through the heart of the city's center. The marines assigned to that section of the cordon waved their hands up and down to instruct the driver to stop, but the blinding of the setting sun made it nearly impossible for the marines to see the driver or for the driver to see them. As the driver approached, a warning shot was fired from an M16 in hopes this would clue in the driver he needed to stop his vehicle immediately as to indicate he was not be some type of insurgent. The shot put the driver in a panic, and he dramatically increased his speed. Directly in his path was a 240 Gulf machine gun being manned by a twenty-one-year-old Lance Corporal David Whitehead, of rural Colorado. Whitehead was six months short of the end of his enlistment, with plans to attend Colorado State University on the GI Bill and avoid the path of working in the Western Colorado coal mines, which so many of his high school classmates had taken. Whitehead locked in his sights as the vehicle raced closer and closer to his position; simultaneously, he was praying the vehicle would stop. He knew this was what he was trained to do, but he also knew the damage a 7.62-millimeter projectile launched from a 240 Gulf machine gun could do to a human body. *What if this guy is just confused? What if he is just scared?*

Alas, the young warrior had to make a choice and act on the assumption the vehicle was a moving IED launcher, a vehicle-borne IED, and the driver's goal was to blow up as many marines as possible. Finally, Whitehead locked in and fired and blew apart the windshield of the small truck. The vehicle jerked to the left and slowed down to a crawl before rolling perfectly right side up into a ditch less than fifty feet away from a family anxiously awaiting their father and grandfather's arrival for a dinner meeting planned that night. Stevie and Hospital Corpsman Rodney Baut were the first to reach the vehicle and check for life or weapons. No one told them to do this, but they thought if it was an IED, it would have blown by now. When the pair looked in the driver's side window they were horrified to see what remained of a fifty-something-year-old man, who now had a torso but not much of a head. The two saddened veterans instantly knew this was a mistake.

"Can you do anything for him?" Stevie asked of Baut.

"He doesn't have a head, Stevie. He doesn't have a head!"

The pair both looked down at the ground, not knowing what do to do next, and failed to notice the panicked approach of four local men who had instantly appeared in front of the truck with the look of horror in their eyes. As Stevie and Baut lifted their weapons to point at the men, they quickly were met with shaking of heads and eyes focused on the body in the truck.

The men did not have to speak a word to communicate they were not armed and had no ill intentions. They only wanted to grab their friend and neighbor from the wreckage and take him away so he could die in the arms of his family. Baut and McClanahan stood back and nodded and granted the men their wish, although knowing good and well he was already dead. The man was dead because he had poor eyesight and had not been able to see the marines warning them. He was dead mainly because they don't have many available optometrists in the western Al Anbar Province!

The limp body was carried across the middle of the courtyard and into a makeshift huddle in front of the dirty little restaurant where the man's family had planned to dine. The marines from all four corners stared helplessly and lost all interest and focus on the vehicle checkpoints they had been tasked with. The marines could also quickly feel the tide of anger and the volume of onlookers rising all around them. Thus, as quickly as the dismounted patrol had begun, it was abruptly aborted. The platoon ran to their vehicles and headed west again, toward their home for the last seven months, Camp Korean Village. No one said a word during the cold ride. It was safe to assume a good number of the shocked marines were thinking, "That could have been my dad. That could have been my grandpa."

There would be no further patrols outside the wire for First Platoon. This tragic event had brought to a close the combat operations for First Platoon, Echo Company, Second Battalion, Seventh Marines, as a part of Operation Iraqi Freedom "Two tack two" (II-2). An investigation was expected, and all the enlisted marines dreaded the thought of being dragged into a huge quagmire when they had done nothing wrong. The dread intensified tenfold when Stevie and Doc Baut was called into Major Horton's office twenty-four hours after the platoon had rolled back into the firebase. Stevie took some relief in the fact he could sense Major Horton did not want to have this conversation any more than he did.

Horton was looking at the deck and occasionally looking up at the two honorable vets. "Baut, what did you do to try and save that man? We have received reports that he was just left to bleed out?"

Baut was distraught and just shook his head as the tears began to stream down his cheek. Doc Baut loved being a greenside navy corpsman. He loved his marines and would do anything for the brothers he had the privilege of serving with. More than anything, however, Rodney Baut valued human life. He chose the Navy Hospital Corps for the purpose of trying to help people who were hurting. Sure, he had to carry a weapon in the combat zone; however, during the entire deployment, he had only fired his weapon a few times, and it was only at vehicle engines when vehicles behind their convoy were getting too close.

Before Hospital Corpsman Third Class Baut could muster a word, Corporal Stephen McClanahan felt the overwhelming need to speak up on both of their behalfs, "Sir, with all due respect, the man's torso was in the driver's seat and his head was in the passenger seat! Sir, there was nothing that could be done. The best doctor in the world wouldn't have been able to save that life."

An awkward silence followed that seemed to last forever until finally, Major Horton removed his hand from his chin and began to slowly nod. "OK, OK, Mac, that's good enough for me. Anyone else asks you questions about this matter, and you tell them the exact same thing, which I believe is the truth."

The two young warriors simultaneously came to attention without prompting and responded with a boisterous *"Yes, sir!"*

"OK, dismissed," stated Horton as a small smile began to form. "Go get some rest and start packing your gear. We are finally getting out of this shithole."

With that, the two now salty veterans exited the tent, feeling a hell of a lot better than they had about their futures only five minutes earlier.

CHAPTER 23

The US military in 2005, like society as a whole, was supposed to be a paperless society, with virtually everything being done electronically. Corporal Theodore Smith, therefore, was required to complete his leave request electronically (or e-Leave for brevity's sake). Despite the fact that Teddy Smith was only about three hours from home and not fit for any type of meaningful duty at the moment, he was undeniably still on active duty and still subject to the rules bestowed upon all other marines regardless of their circumstances. Without complaint, Corporal Smith completed and submitted his e-Leave request on 01 March 2005. He was requesting convalescent or recovery leave at home for twenty-one days before returning to San Antonio to continue his rehabilitation. In the case of convalescent leave, this would need to be recommended by his treating physician and approved by his current chain of command, which was the Brook Army Medical Center.

The idea behind e-Leave was it could be approved quicker and would not sit as hard copy on some commander's desk for weeks while the requestor remained in limbo. Well, good intentions don't always translate to good results, and as of 11 March 2005 Corporal Smith had heard nothing back regarding his request. This was not without good reason in Smitty's particular case. The discussion among the staff at BAMC was how long they could reasonably allow Corporal Smith to deter from his physical therapy and the progress he was making.

In addition, Corporal Smith had shown extreme motivation in both his physical therapy and his overall mood. Smitty made it a habit to visit other wounded vets in adjoining wards almost daily. When he would walk into a room and was told to f—— off, he would respond by saying, "It's OK. I still love you, man, and I will see you tomorrow, motivator!"

Thus the dilemma faced by the chain of command was, what was truly best at this stage for this broken marine? Should he be punished for showing a good attitude and being positive about his situation and positive toward others? In the end it was decided Corporal Smith was stable enough to go home, but twenty-one days would be counterproductive. He would be granted fourteen days of leave, which would begin on 23 March 2005—coincidentally, the same day that Alpha Company was scheduled to depart Iraq en route for the Continental United States.

Alpha Company would depart Camp Korean Village on 12 March 2005 via air and ground. Half the company would travel to Al Asad via helo, and half the company would be stuck on a convoy. The convoy would be a dusty, bumpy, cold, and above all, dangerous ride between Ar Rutbah, Iraq, and Al Asad Air Base, the first stop of the retrograde they had all longed for. By luck of the draw, Stevie fell into the group that would travel via helo. It would still be cold although a lot less dusty and bumpy and a whole lot quicker. As one last insult from the western Al Anbar weather, a rare thunderstorm pounded Camp Korean Village on the evening of 11 March 2005, which made the FOB a virtual mud pit and threatened the outbound helo flights slated for the next morning. The marines in fact were able to depart Camp Korean Village timely on 12 March 2005, but only after having to mop and wipe down mud-infested buildings and tents. This was one working party there would be no bitching and moaning about, as a little mud on the cammies wasn't going to dampen the spirits of a single warrior from Echo 2/7. The worries of the ground convoy coming into contact with undesirables in route did not come to fruition, and six hours after the last Echo vehicle departed Camp Ar Rutbah, all Echo Company was present *and* accounted for, safely aboard Al Asad Air Base. Retrograde had officially begun!

Other than cleaning weapons, the company had little responsibility for the next week, and that was fine with them. There would be the first of many seabag gear dumps to check for contraband, but beyond that, the weary troopers were allowed to sleep in, shower, work out, and eat, eat, eat in the deluxe Halliburton chow halls located on the sprawling air base. The troopers were told to expect a week-plus stay at Al Asad before moving on to Kuwait, but instead they received word to pack up on the night of 16 March 2005, as they were catching an Air Force C-130 to Kuwait on Friday morning, 17 March. Not surprisingly, no one complained about the lack of notice, as Kuwait was one step closer to the "the Land of the Big PX," a.k.a. the USA.

As much as they tried, no one could sleep a wink on the night of 16 March as they all had something to look forward to upon arrival back in

CONUS. Even the warriors without wives and kids were fired up about taking off the cammies for a couple of weeks of leave and going on a trip to their hometown or Vegas or, oddly enough, *camping*! It never fails that marines can load seabags on a homeward-bound flight a hell of a lot faster than a deployment-bound flight. This time, there were sergeants and even staff sergeants helping pass seabags into the underbelly of the plane. The sooner the plane took off, the better, as Echo Company did not want to give the higher-ups any time to change their mind regarding their departure date. The plane was airborne by 0900, and by 1100, Echo Company was in their tents at Camp Victory, surrounded by a Pizza Hut, a Subway, and a Baskin-Robbins Ice Cream shop. No one in flak jackets or Kevlar helmets, and no obvious clues anywhere they were one country away from a raging war zone.

Once again, the marines had very little responsibility other than keeping track of their rifles and keeping them clean. Kuwait wasn't ridiculously hot in March; however, it was still dusty, and there were still concerns about dehydration and marines getting in trouble via black market alcohol. The marines had to deal with a few more daily formations; however, they all understood, as they could not risk losing a man at this stage, and there is nothing more frustrating and regrettable than a noncombat injury. They received confidential word that they would be flying through the Shannon, Ireland, airport on the way home but could not be given an exact date or time they would be stateside as of yet for OPSEC purposes. The scuttlebutt was that the battalion commander (BC) would allow the troops to have a few beers in the Shannon, Ireland, airport bar, and the "on the way home" adult beverages would taste almost as sweet as the welcome home beverages stateside. They were still officially dry for now, and any booze found in seabags in Kuwait would mean a marine or sailor would be standing before the man (the BC)! It was getting hot anyway, and the marines were just enjoying the endless chow and cold nonalcoholic drinks that were readily available at Camp Victory. The marines formed up on the evening of 21 March 2003 and were told to shower and pack everything that evening and to be ready to shave and thoroughly clean their tents at 0400 on 22 March prior to boarding buses at 0500, which would depart for the flight line. Marines routinely went without showers when circumstances dictated, but rarely were they allowed taking a day off from shaving. The order also went out to marines who had let their hair grow out that they were not getting on the "freedom bird" home until they had a proper regulation United States Marine Corps haircut.

As expected, the weary jarheads who had longed for the day when they could get a good night's sleep were unable to fall asleep at all the night before flying home, just like children the night before Christmas. Under a calm, cloudless sky in a relatively cool Kuwait desert, the temporary tents and heads at the marine berthing area of Camp Victory were made to be as pristine as they had ever been. Shortly thereafter, the seabag loading aboard the five-ton trucks and, subsequently, the huge chartered World Airlines jet was done in record time. As the bird finally went airborne shortly after 0800, the exhaustion of seven long months of fear and homesickness, anger and sadness began to take its toll. The raucous jet was filled with exuberance for the first fifty to fifty-five minutes of the long and happy flight, but then, like a switch had been flipped, it was instantly quiet. Nearly 100 percent of Echo Company and half of Headquarters Company, also aboard, drifted into a deep sleep—a deep, happy sleep. They were at last headed in the right direction, westward bound.

CHAPTER 24

About the same time the freedom bird was going vertical, across the world in Harbor Lake, Texas, the humidity and the excitement were increasing by the day. Bill and Connie Smith were about to welcome their son back to his very own bedroom in the house he adored and the only home outside the Marine Corps he had ever known. It was only for two weeks; however, it was to be the best two weeks they have ever known. Nothing in the world seemed to matter—not the war, not debt, not Bill's aching back; nothing. They would have their son back for a while, and everything would be right with the world. Bill and Connie would travel to San Antonio on 22 March to pick up their beloved boy, who was still not cleared to drive, and begin the wonderful three-hour drive back home down Interstate 10. Connie had to keep reminding Bill they would need to take their time and not get into a car accident, coming or going. They had been through enough, an extra thirty minutes wasn't going to kill them!

Teddy had signed out for leave and stood waiting outside the BAMC barracks for what seemed like hours. When his parents arrived, they wanted to take him out for dinner before getting back on the road. Their weary son wanted no part of that as he was ready to see his childhood home and take a nap in his old bed. He politely declined the invitation by telling his mother, "Mom, I have been craving your cooking for the longest time. Let's go home." There was no argument from Mom as she longed to have her son under her roof again, if only for a few daysBa. One hour into the trip, however, Teddy spotted a Whataburger, a famous Texas fast-food joint, on the side of I-10 and requested they make a quick pit stop. So many times in Iraq, he had longed for a good burger from Whataburger and discussed this often with his buddy Stevie via e-mail. Teddy had not left the grounds of BAMC much since he had been back in Texas and thus still had not had the flat burgers and mouthwatering fries from the famous orange-and-white stripe-decorated restaurants. Part of Teddy wanted to go through the drive through and keep on pace for a timely arrival home, but part of him wanted to dine inside the restaurant and smell the wonderful grill and the pure aroma of fresh french fries that always filled the air. On the suggestion of his dear old dad, they compromised and walked inside but had the food to go.

When they got back on the road, the sweet childhood memories starting entering Teddy's mind, as he remembered so many trips to Whataburger after baseball games as a child. As Teddy stared out the window, he began to slowly form a smile and drift off to sleep. His mother, Connie, filled with goose bumps due to having her son return home again, began to smile as her son faded into Dreamland, and her wonderful memories began to come back as well.

Teddy's perfectly timed nap ended as his eyes automatically popped open, right on cue, as the Smith family turned onto Woodbank Drive in Harbor Lake, Texas. Teddy loved his house on 1007 Woodbank. It was the only home he had ever lived in prior to the Marine Corps, and to him, it looked like a mansion. He had never really understood why people needed five-thousand- or ten-thousand-square-foot homes. Two thousand had always seemed like more than enough. He had recently heard that football star Tom Brady had moved into a thirty-thousand-square-foot house, and that made Teddy nauseous! How many orphanages could be built with thirty thousand square feet? As the car pulled into the old driveway they had pulled into thousands of times before, Mom, Dad, and son were all smiles. No words were spoken, and none needed to be. If anyone was to say something, the only words that would be appropriate would be Dorothy's from *The Wizard of Oz*, "There's no place like home, and there's *no* place like home."

J. P. McClanahan had been updating his son Stevie regarding the travel plans of his longtime buddy and fellow marine. As happy as Stevie was to be in the air, headed west toward CONUS, he was even happier for his buddy, whom he knew would be sleeping in his old high school bed tonight. Stevie knew deep down how good he had it growing up in Harbor Lake, yet a little time in the Middle East had reminded him of how lucky he had been to have a nice roof over his head with perks such as air conditioning and running water. *My god*, he thought, *how in the hell do people anywhere not have running water in the year 2005?* Most of all, however, he felt so damn lucky for all the good times he had been a part of—great parents, great neighbors, great friends, and great memories. Additionally, he felt so damn lucky to have been a Harbor Lake Falcon and playing right beside a local legend.

He also knew deep down, his old friend needed to get back into baseball somehow. Stevie just could not see Teddy making a living in any other form or fashion. If his injuries were as bad as he had heard though, a playing career was likely out of the question. Maybe they could attend college together at Texas State or Texas Tech and become coaches and teachers. Smitty hated the classroom although never seemed to mind when Stevie tutored him. If anyone else called him stupid, he would become enraged. Stevie, on the other hand, could rag him all day long, and Teddy would just take it, knowing his friend always had his best interests at heart.

When Teddy Smith walked through the front door of his home, it was as if he had never left. Everything was in the same exact place, and everything smelled exactly the same. He loved how clean his mom always kept their home and was easily disgusted with other people's homes (much like his germa-phone dad). Bill had always been extremely organized to the point of being anal, and therefore, all the books and furniture in the house remained at precisely the same angle with the same spacing as Teddy had remembered. He took comfort in the fact that despite all that had changed in his life, some things definitely remained the same.

The Smith family, unlike many families in 2005, actually still had a home phone, and inevitably, just as Teddy had become comfortable and was dozing off, the phone rang and scared the hell out of him. It was quickly picked up by Bill, who knew his son was trying to nap, and Teddy began to immediately doze back off as, surely, the call couldn't be for him.

The Smiths had told a few very close relatives and friends that their son would be coming home soon for a visit but had been careful not to share any specific dates. Bill knew he shouldn't shake his son from sleep after what he had been through, yet he knew his son would want to talk to this particular caller. Bill asked the caller on the line to be patient, and Bill turned on the stereo in Teddy's old room, which remained tuned to Classic Rock 107.5, and watched his son's eyes slowly reopen while a grimace formed on his face.

Once Teddy's eyes were fully open and he had his dad in full view, he became concerned. "What is it, Dad? What's the matter?"

Teddy's apprehension quickly disappeared as he saw the smile forming on his dad's face. Bill did not answer the question; instead he just handed the portable phone to his son.

Before Teddy had a chance to utter the word *hello*, his old friend of nearly two decades lit into him, "Really, Smith, really? This is how you thank the taxpayers of this country who pay your salary, by going home and taking naps instead of trying to get healthy?"

Teddy shook his head in amazement as this was the last person he expected to hear from at this very moment, not even knowing where in the world his old buddy was. "Well, if it isn't the worst hitter in Harbor Lake history," Smitty retorted. "Where the hell are you, shitbird?"

"I'm in Shannon, Ireland, you bastard, having a green beer on my way home. Someone has to come back and motivate you non-hackers!"

With this, Smitty could not help but laugh, and when he did, his bones ached. His foot and hand had taken the brunt of the blast; however, residual soreness radiated from head to toe with any sudden movements. After the two shared a laugh, a respectful but awkward silence followed, and Stevie Mac knew it was time to turn serious. "Hey, bud, we will be back in the Stumps [Twentynine Palms] by tomorrow. I'll be home in a week, and I'll come see you."

Smitty choked up a little bit as he replied, "Yeah, you do that, man. You come see me, brother. It's damn good to hear your voice. It will be good to have you back, old friend."

Stevie also struggled getting the words out as he knew his friend was hurting and he didn't want to downplay that. He was nodding into the phone receiver, trying to find a way to end the conversation on a high note. As the officers and senior NCOs in the background began to go through the bar, yelling at the marines to drop their drink and head to the plane, Teddy heard the emotion in Stevie's voice as he forced out, "I'll see you soon, you stubborn bastard. I'll see you *soon!*"

One would expect a plane full or marines, with a few sailors sprinkled in, who had just had a few adult beverages to be mighty rowdy. Yet to a man, all hands slipped into a happy daydream state or else fell asleep altogether while dreaming happy thoughts. Everyone aboard felt so blessed, so lucky to be returning to what they considered the greatest country on earth. They all ached for the people of the Middle East, and none understood why the region had been so damn screwed up for so long, yet they knew they had done what they could during their recent time in the region and were heading back to CONUS with a mostly clear conscience.

Twentynine Palms, California, had seen its share of welcome home celebrations before. The days of people from neighboring towns such as Joshua Tree or Yucca Valley lining the streets with American Flags and screaming for the returning troops as they passed through on buses were long gone. As the marines and sailors of Second Battalion, Seventh Marine Regiment, rolled through, the streets were empty, and there wasn't as much as a single sign on a storefront window with welcome home wishes. The entire country, and especially the military towns outside installations, had grown weary of war after two years of simultaneous conflicts in Afghanistan and Iraq. The inhabitants of the 2/7 busses did not have hurt feelings and seemed to be more relieved than offended they were returning home quietly. Everyone in the battalion knew someone who had been either wounded or killed. Many had witnessed their friends being blown up firsthand, and thus, a time for celebration didn't seem appropriate now or in the near future. As the procession turned onto the two-mile road that dead-ended into the *Marine Air Ground Combat Center Twentynine Palms*, signs (literal signs) began to appear along the fence that lined the unpopulated road. One sign that brought a chuckle to the warriors on the busses, especially the married marines and sailors, read "DESPERATE HOUSEWIVES NO MORE! WELCOME HOME, M-E-N OF 2/7!"

As it turns out, nearly every marine and sailor had a visible sign bearing their name along the fence somewhere, an extraordinary effort by the Key Volunteer Club led by marine spouses on the base. This again supported the popular and largely accurate conclusion there really wasn't a much tighter community to be found than active duty military dependents inhabiting in and around a military base, especially during time of the war. Twentynine Palms, California, being what it was, more of a meth lab than a military town, led to most families living on base and making the remote family atmosphere of Twentynine Stumps even tighter.

As the caravan actually entered the gates of the base, there was no sign of life anywhere, and the boys began to wonder if the rear echelon of 2/7 had misinformed the families about the arrival time and date of the elements of the battalion that were arriving home today (three of the five companies were coming home tomorrow with only Echo plus H&S slated to arrive today). The buses then took an upward turn toward the main parade ground, and then the faces came alive and the electricity was instant. A dirt-filled playground and soccer field—which looked out of place, like many structures at Twentynine Palms—was completely overpopulated with wives, kids, parents, and grandparents. The buses screeched to a halt along the picket fence surrounding the recreation area. Any attempt by the leadership to conduct an orderly procession off the bus was abandoned to the wolves as they knew their marines had waited long enough to let their guard down.

As Stephen McClanahan exited the bus, he smiled as he saw marines and sailors he knew seek out and find their loved ones and enjoy bear hugs galore. Stevie was mentally prepared for the fact that his folks were not going to make it out as he had told them the homecoming could wait a weekend. Twentynine Palms was certainly not an easy place to get to.

As the younger McClanahan shuffled off the stairs of the bus, he noticed a long rectangular sign out of the corner of his eye. The white cardboard sign had lettering spelled out in red Magic Marker, with each letter outlined in Blue, and read "MY MAC IS BACK!" At the moment, Stevie noticed the sign, it began to lower, and a grinning face came into view—the unmistakable grin belonged to none other than Betty Lou McClanahan, his relieved mother, who was not going to wait one more second for this well-deserved reunion with her beloved son. The overwhelmed son was speechless and filled with overwhelming gratitude as he hugged his mom and thanked her for making the effort to travel to the Mojave Desert, and this hug was before he even knew Mom could not find a flight and had *driven* the twenty-three hours from Southeast Texas to Southeast California by herself. Betty informed her son his dad wanted to make the trip, but while not crazy about Mom traveling by herself, he had wanted to stay home in order to plan and set up for Stevie's welcome home party in Harbor Lake, Texas.

Over the next four to five days, mother and son did not have much chance to see each other as the marines were busy in debriefs and post deployment processing from early morning into the evening in addition to daily weapons cleaning. No worry to Mom, however, as she prepared food at the Little Turtle Navy Lodge at Twentynine Palms and had some home cooking ready for Stevie every night. Mom headed back to Texas on Tuesday, sad but excited, knowing her son would be several days behind her when the battalion was granted block leave on 01 April. Mom promised husband JP and son Stephen she would only drive on the return trip during daylight hours and expand the trip to 2.5 days, staying overnight twice. Therefore, once Betty Lou pulled into her driveway in Harbor Lake, Stevie's flight would only be one day behind her. Stevie was a little sad to see her go and a little worried about the drive she was about to make, yet her departure meant he could finally let loose with the warriors he had trained, fought, and lived with for most of the previous year. The battalion was granted off-base liberty but was not authorized to travel as far as Palm Springs, which meant Twentynine Palms, Yucca Valley, or Joshua Tree, California, none of which offered much in the way of entertainment or were overwhelmingly friendly to marines (or sailors). As a result, the strong majority of the base made the wise move and stayed on base and away from motorized vehicles. No one wanted to get in trouble for fighting or, especially, drinking and driving when a trip home on leave for all was on the horizon.

On 28 May 2005, Corporal Stephen McClanahan climbed in his 2001 Honda Civic and began the trip east to Texas to enjoy fourteen days of post deployment leave. He took some abuse from most of the guys in the unit, but his Civic ran beautifully, had ridiculously good gas mileage, and he was able to pay it off in full while deployed. Since he had hassled his mom about stopping, Stevie agreed to not drive straight through the night and would drive only to Las Cruces, New Mexico, on his first night.

On 29 March 2005, he would quickly cross over the Texas Border into El Paso. He was in his home state at last, yet with Texas being insanely wide, eight hundred plus miles still remained on the trip, which meant eleven hours of drive time, assuming one drove at a reasonable rate. Stevie had carpooled in the past, but this time around, other Texans were flying or driving home with family. He liked the solitude and enjoyed taking his time. He knew he would get home late on 29 March; however, he would get there alive, have a steak at home off the McClanahan backyard grill, and then rest up for his welcome home party on Saturday, 30 March 2005.

CHAPTER 25

Stevie pulled into his driveway on Crownwood Drive in Harbor Lake, Texas, at 8:05 p.m. on 29 March 2005, about an hour before he had told his dad he would arrive. Dear old Dad knew his son too well and therefore brought a lawn chair out to the front yard about 7:30 to enjoy a beer and listen to some music and anxiously watch for his son to come driving down the street.

As Stevie pulled in, he saw a smile as big as Texas forming on his dad's face, and it gave him goose bumps. What a wonderful feeling to be missed and loved so much. Not expecting to see his dad in the front yard, he quickly turned down his car radio, which was blasting way too loud, and threw the door open, almost forgetting to put the car in park before jumping out. Not a word was said as the two men slowly approached each other. As they got closer, both dad and son tried to force words out, but common sense told them nothing was more appropriate right now than a big bear hug, which really said it all.

Finally JP was able to utter "Welcome home, son," to which Stevie was able to get out a reply despite a big lump in his throat. "I missed you, Dad. I missed our house. This is my favorite place on earth!" They then heard a tap on the dining room window which overlooked the front yard; Mom was waving them in vigorously.

"Mom just started some spaghetti with the garlic bread you love. Let's go inside and fill our bellies." This definitely made Stevie smile.

Ah, the simple things in life like home cooking! After gorging himself on the delicious pasta and bread and a couple of Dad's ice-cold beers, the combat-hardened marine nearly fell asleep at the table. His mom walked him up the stairs and untucked his sheets just like she had so many times when he was a small boy. Dad then walked in the room and informed him,

"You can sleep in for a while, tough guy, but we have someone we need to go see in the morning."

"Who's that?" pondered a worn-out Stevie.

"No big deal. Just someone who has a little surprise for you."

Stevie was too worn out to force the issue any further, and the marine came out in him—"Roger that, sir"—and he was then out before his head hit the pillow.

Across town, corporal Theodore "Teddy" Smith was enjoying his mother's beef stroganoff he loved so much while dozing off to the movie *Fletch*, a quirky comedy he had watched a thousand times which always cheered him up. Normally Connie would never let him eat or sleep in the living room, but he was being cut some serious slack these days after all he had been through. Before his eyes lids completely shut, his dad casually told him, "We need to go over to the ball field in the morning. Coach Ferrell really wants to see you."

Smitty let out a little smile and responded, "Sure, Dad. That sounds all right. It will be good to see Coach." And with that, he was out for the night, snoring almost instantly.

When morning came in Harbor Lake, two dads in adjacent neighborhoods were urging their grown sons to finish their breakfast so they could be on their way to the high school. Stevie pressed his dad, wanting to know who they were going to meet, and JP momentarily panicked. Finally remembering Coach Ferrell would be meeting them as well, he cleverly mused, "Coach Ferrell wants to run you through some drills for fun, see if you still know how to play the game."

A little suspicious yet also excited, Stevie had to ask, "Why does he want to do this at 0830 in the morning? Coach never struck me as a morning person."

Dad was ready this time. "Coach is taking one of his current players on a recruiting trip today, so he wanted to see you before your homecoming week becomes too busy."

Simultaneously, Bill Smith was reciting his well-rehearsed lines to his own beloved son en route to Spartan Field. In response to Teddy's protest that he would like to swing by Stevie's house as opposed to being anywhere else, Bill, on cue, replied, "I promise we'll swing by the McClanahan's place right after we see Coach Ferrell."

All right, that sounds fair enough, thought Teddy. He did, in fact, want to see grumpy old Coach Ferrell and did think very highly of the man, and although he would have rather seen Stevie first, visiting his old coach seemed like the respectable thing to do.

The McClanahans arrived first, and JP advised Stevie he had forgotten to pick up breakfast tacos as he had promised Coach Ferrell.

"I'll be right back. Just hang out in the dugout, and I'll be right back. Coach will be here any minute."

Stevie remained a little suspicious of it all, yet breakfast tacos sounded mighty nice about now. There were no Taco Cabana restaurants in Iraq, and the tacos brought back so many good memories of Saturday mornings after a big Friday night game and a postgame party. With perfect timing, as if it had been rehearsed for months, the Ford Ranger with Bill Smith and his son, Teddy, pulled alongside the field just as the vehicle occupied by J. P. McClanahan drove away.

Bill Smith said "To hell with the parking lot" and drove slowly through the Spartan football practice fields right up behind the dugout of Spartan Field.

As Stevie saw them approaching, he braced himself, knowing he was about to see his friend in a somewhat broken state and not wanting this to show in his face. Despite attempts to prepare himself, Stevie could not maintain his smile as he watched his lifelong friend slowly exit the vehicle and open the gate outside the third base dugout.

Stevie was taken aback by how skinny Teddy had become and was trying to collect himself when Smitty broke the awkward silence. "What the hell are you doing here? You still daydreaming about trying to hit a curveball?"

With that, Stevie's face lit up, and he retorted, "Welcome home, you cocky son of a bitch, and by the way, you are *not* invited to the party tonight."

The two now salty veterans reached out to shake hands as they were both shaken by a booming voice screaming in their direction. "Hey, get off my field, you slackers!" It was none other than Coach Jimmy Ferrell speed walking across the infield after coming out of nowhere. Coach was on them in no time, giving out several bear hugs while dip rolled down his always scruffy three-day beard. "Welcome home, welcome home, welcome home" was all he could repeat over and over.

Before his two former players could respond, they noticed a nicely groomed, bearded man in pristine khakis and a pressed blue polo pullover with a Nike swoosh and the words Rice Baseball above the left breast pocket. Ferrell noticed the boys' reaction to the stranger and began laughing. "Shit, I almost forgot. I have somebody I want you boys to meet. This is Johnny Kaminski from the Rice Baseball staff."

That's nice, the two buddies thought, *but what is this guy doing out here interrupting a private, emotional moment?*

As if reading their mind, Kaminski began to address the two young men with a very respectful tone. "Gentlemen, I apologize for interrupting this private reunion, but I was curious if you two still had interest in playing college baseball?" Again anticipating their pending questions, Kaminski continued, "I know you're still in the Marine Corps"—he looked at Stevie—"and I know you're hurt"—he looked at Teddy. "Neither of you has signed a pro contract, and neither of you has used a day of eligibility. The fact is, we have a few guys who will be seniors this year and a few more juniors who are going to sign pro contracts. Come next summer, '06, we are going to need some guys who can commit to us for four years. I figure, Stevie, you want the degree, and, Teddy, you need some time to get that stroke and your body back. I can offer you both half scholarships and financial aid for the remainder. What do you think?"

The boys were stunned and looked to Coach Ferrell for some type of clue as to what to say next. "Gents," Ferrell stated, "your parents know all about this, and they're all for it. I think you would be crazy not to take Rice up on this offer. Hell, they have been going to the College World Series almost every year!"

Stevie was ready to say yes on the spot, but again, before he could muster a word, Kaminski came with his grand finale. "You guys are no longer in high school, and we're not breaking any rules by offering you a couple seats with us on the plane to Omaha this summer for the College World Series. So can you let us know by then?"

"Yes, sir, yes, sir," they both finally repeated, not being able to come up with anything more clever or historic.

"Good deal, I'll talk to you gents soon. Coach Ferrell has my contact info when you're ready."

With that, the sharp-dressed Kaminski was gone and headed back to the Rice campus, feeling good about what he had just done.

The normally wise-ass Ferrell, who never let people see him cry, was obviously choked up and, with a lump in this throat, advised his two pupils, "Go see your families. I'll see you two chumps tonight." Turning serious, he left them with "I'm so damn glad you're alive. You're good kids—I mean *men*. You're good men." Then with a nod, he turned and walked away, and the pair looked toward the parking lot where both dads were watching from a distance with big smiles on their faces.

"Why in the hell would Rice University want a chump like you who can't hit a curveball?" cracked Smitty.

"Why the hell would they want a moron who can't even read?" Stevie responded.

"Come on. Let's go get some tacos, devil dog," a tearing-up Smitty advised.

"Tacos, a scholarship offer, and a party with old buddies. Today might not be that bad of a day," Stevie said as he put his arm around his skinny, hobbling old buddy.

"I've had worse, bud. I've had worse, Stevie. Now let's get ready to party Spartan style!"